MAX SEES RED

Martha King

SPUYTEN DUYVIL

NEW YORK CITY

This book is a work of fiction. Names, characters, places, and incidents are the product of the author's imagination or are used fictitiously. Any resemblance to actual events or persons living or dead is coincidental.

However, the author would like to thank many friends and associates for fueling the creation of events and characters found in this book. I couldn't have invented all of it without inspiration.

ISBN 978-1-949966-06-0

Library of Congress Cataloging-in-Publication Data

Names: King, Martha, author.
Title: Max sees red / Martha King.
Description: New York City : Spuyten Duyvil, [2019]
Identifiers: LCCN 2018053145 | ISBN 9781949966060
Classification: LCC PS3561.I4817 M39 2019 | DDC 813/.54—dc23
LC record available at https://lccn.loc.gov/2018053145

To the seven or more BHK's, with my love

I'm just a little younger now than my mother was on the day she died. I have only the cloudiest memories of her. In fact, most of them are questionable, all muddied by what people have told me, photos I've looked at and my own fantasies. I'll let the neurochemists and psychiatrists duke out if what I have is memory or not. I have facts, that's sure. I have them now. The biggest is the fact that my mother was taken from me by violence. She was horribly killed. I've gone into, not away from it, and imagined her death in cold detail. I've imagined her killers, too. But the second biggest fact I have is that I don't have to wonder about who they were or why they did what they did because their motives and the consequences have unfolded in the years since the fire on Horse Creek Road. A very odd set of circumstances led to me getting the story whole, that is, whole enough to be told as a story. The girots know that story is how history is carried. I think the burden I carry would be a great deal heavier if I didn't have these facts.

My mother was not only my mother, she was my white side, the side that doesn't show. We're instant black, all us mulattoes, and then we have to put up with white people insisting that we understand and forgive them because somehow we're white (we must be) even though we are not! That work is another story—mine. This story is the one I owe to Max. He's an unlikely hero, for sure. He was not my mother's friend, and not mine, not then or now. Just the same I owe him. I think it's richly funny that he's now so art-world famous because he's famous to me for very different reasons.

Sidney Albassa, Los Angeles, 2013

A Death on Horse Creek Road, 1978

In the pool of light from a high intensity lamp a woman moved four piles of paper. The smallest pile, to her left, was face down and cross-ribbed with strips of yellow paper. She read a page from the right-hand pile rapidly, her pencil poised over the lines. As she reached the bottom she compulsively straightened the heap, then turned a new page in the third pile face up. She compared the two. Her lips pursed tight. She pulled a curled wisp of fine brown hair out from her temple and turned it firmly behind her ear.

An empty twig ticked against the sunroom roof.

She looked up.

The rest of the room was in semi-darkness. She and her worktable reflected on the black surfaces of a window wall above the day bed. The repeated images glittered irregularly from pane to pane. Windows from three or four superannuated farmhouses had been fastened together to make it.

The branch banged harder against the roof and the gas furnace in the crawl space below rumbled and kicked on.

The woman looked annoyed. It must be blowing up. The house was imperfectly insulated and even with its newly acquired automatic furnace it would be impossible to warm if the temperature dipped in earnest. She pushed back in her chair, massaging her neck, and, in spite of herself, began another mental list of things that needed doing here. It was a kind of shack, this place; but its drawbacks were part of its charm weren't they? She frowned with worry, looking back at the table again where a half-eaten container of manicotti sat on the open rack of the toaster oven. She picked it up and walked up three uneven steps and across the narrow hall.

It was warmer in the kitchen. The overhead light she pulled on glowed harshly across the old linoleum and the jerrybuilt shelves that held her motley second-hand pots and plates. She grinned suddenly, thinking of the contrast with her sleek chrome-and-wood city kitchenette, realizing, as she smiled, that she should stop turning around in an aimless circle.

"Shoo," she said out loud. "I'm really bushed."

She wrapped the container in plastic and placed it in the refrigerator next to the milk, eggs, bread and coffee she'd brought with her. The watch on her wrist was nearly as large as a silver dollar. It said 11:32. She turned the kitchen light off and went back to the hall but instead of returning to the worktable in the sunroom she opened the front door. It led to a high rickety deck from which a flight of steps descended to a gravel drive and the garage where she had locked her car. It was blowing up. Above the bare trees, a quarter moon raced with torn scuds of gray-black cloud. There were no lights anywhere. She looked down the long meadow to the road, past the dark trees along the creek and toward the twisted hedge by the road. The Pattelsons had moved out of the little house right by the road and she hoped whoever took the place come summer would not give all-night parties. People with children she hoped; Siddy would miss Jimbo Pattelsohn.

It was cold. She could hear the creek, gorged with spring snowmelt. She latched the door. In the sunroom she looked resignedly at the four piles and the canvas tote bag on the day bed bulging with still more paper. She turned out this light too and fumbled up the dark stairs to the attic floor *where two small bedrooms and a tiny bath were wedged against the slanted roof. The wind was louder. One of the windows was rattling. She remembered she'd forgotten to turn the thermostat down to 65 and her sense of thrift was slightly aggravated because she'd no intention of going back downstairs to fix it. Damn furnace'll work all night and the place will still be freezing in the morning, she thought.*

As she went through her bedtime routines, she began to feel all the abuse of the day. Her legs and shoulders ached woodenly from the tension of parkway traffic. You're 38 years old, she told herself, it's time you had respect for that. As she squirmed into the slightly damp, musty smelling bed, her head clanged with images of the day—a last-minute race to tie up enough loose ends to make two days out of town possible. Two projects, both in trouble, a stream of people she should be seeing, and now this place, she thought with growing irritability. My lovely kick-your-shoes-off-in-the-country hideaway—it's a dump, a wreck. Fix one thing and three other things break down. I'm a fool for buying it, she yelled inside herself, throwing my money down this rat hole. What's wrong with me?

She sat up suddenly, wondering if she should take a Valium. Can't risk being muzzy, she decided. I want the whole day for work. For work. She lay back again, trying to focus on her yoga mantra. For work, for work circled around her instead. Work that would not get done.

#

Something was in the driveway. Her eyes flew open; not the wind, not the rattling window. The travel alarm on the bedside table glowed green. It was not quite one a.m. None of the attic windows gave on the front of the house. The woman tiptoed across the room and pressed her face against the windowpane. Dark trees, dark night. Were raccoons in the garbage pails? But the pails were locked in the storeroom under the sunroom. Was that voices?

A kind of light from the front of the house seemed to leak up the hill and glow raggedly on the bushes above. She stood in the dark, in bare feet, on a cold wood floor, and felt herself begin to sweat. It was voices. Male voices. Calling to each other.

Mitzi had been furious at her lack of a bedside telephone. Anger at herself surged against her fear. She fumbled in her suitcase for her heavy bathrobe. The phone was downstairs in the sunroom, on the floor under the worktable.

Sounds of clanging and crackling were louder when she opened her bedroom door.

"Jesus Christ, look at her climb!" a voice shouted ecstatically.

Cheers. Clapping.

It wasn't dark on the narrow stairs. A dusty-rose flicker lit the sunroom windows. The woman walked faster, mechanically turning lights on as she moved: the hall light, the switch for the deck outside, the sun room overhead, the reading lamp by the day bed. Hands shielding eyes, she looked out. Against the illumination now spilling from her windows a smoky sunrise glow changed to billows of dirty browns and grays. A coil of clear flame twisted the length of one deck support, bright as a Halloween lantern.

For long seconds she stuck to the window, screaming. Then she rocked back on the day bed and pushed both hands through the glass.

"Oh what!" She got the words out as warm blood ran down her left arm. There was a jagged cut up the fleshy part of her forearm. Her right arm was unscratched.

The cheering had stopped. Now the voices shouted and cursed. A figure ran to a van which was parked facing down the hill, and ran back again, leaving the cab door open.

"Do it! Do it!" shrilled the highest voice. "She's gonna blow!"

"Damn it!"

"NO, DON'T!"

Two figures seemed to be grappling.

Choking smoke poured in through the broken glass. The woman pulled her hands inside carefully, looking at them as if examining foreign curios. She knew she was still screaming. Like a scarecrow, she held her arms out from her sides and ran for the latched front door. She could hear the dry deck supports snapping as they caught. Out! Get out.

Before she reached the door it broke open. He was holding something shiny in his upraised left hand. She knew him.

Her mouth closed over her scream. She whirled aiming for the attic stairs, tossing an arc of blood from her torn arm. Her bathrobe tripped her. Her knees crashed heavily against the bottom step and she felt her fingernails breaking in the wooden tread before the first blow caught the left side of her skull.

Max knew he wasn't drowning but he went on doggedly thrashing. The crazed clanging of the *Cleveland Johnson's* alarm bell began to resolve itself: the telephone. He struggled for breath. He was not gasping the Gulf waters off Biloxi. Pale blue death, the rust-busted tanker's squealing agonies cleared as he freed himself from the warm bedding. The phone, clearly the telephone, ringing across the loft like a cry.

Propped on his elbows he looked down from the bed platform. Betsy's white legs and sleep-rosy butt pattered purposefully across the shiny boards toward the alcove and the ringing phone. It had been a lot of years and she was.... His pleasure sank. Traffic noise five flights below was already at mid-morning volume. He could hear diesel motors gasp and boom as trucks maneuvered on the narrow street. The whole building throbbed perceptibly in response. The clock said half-past ten. Damn.

"Oh Lynn, my god, no!" Betsy's voice was shrill.

Max sat up, ice knotting in his gut. She looked up at him desperately, and made sharp, inconclusive gestures with her hands: shhhh! no! come quick!

"How did it happen?"

Max hit just one ladder rung on his way down, grabbed for the robe on a clothes peg under the platform, helped her into it as she dexterously switched phone ears.

"Yeah, yeah," she said. "Oh Jesus." Her eyes were full of tears as she looked up at Max.

"Just a sec," she said into the phone. "It's Shirley

Pendergast," she told him. "She's dead. Her house caught fire. Her country house." She turned back to the phone. "Does Siddy know?" And then, "Listen, Lynn, I'm coming over. Just let me get my clothes on. I'll be there in an hour."

She wiped her eyes on the sleeve of the robe. Max held her, putting his nose into the wonderfully rich live smell of her brown hair.

"Hey, hey," he said, feeling enormous guilty relief. Shirley Pendergast; it could be a lot worse.

Strong sunshine slanted through the bamboo blinds at the south end of the loft, striping the hanging pots of herbs and ferns. Light formed dots on the row of wooden stools he and Betsy had painted lavender, yellow, pale green, and orange. He led Betsy to one of the stools and lit the gas under the kettle.

"God," he said, "horrible way."

Betsy blew her nose on a crumbled Kleenex and folded it with shaking fingers.

"It happened last night sometime. She doesn't usually go up there on a weekday. But she had a lot of work to catch up on. A big new book. Sometime last night.... They don't know how it started. Siddy's with them. She left Siddy with Lynn and Mitzi. Oh Max," she burst, tears running again, "that poor kid, what's she gonna do?"

"You going over there?"

"They're just hysterical," Betsy answered as she controlled herself. "Well, I know I can help some way." Her pale face settled itself, though tears continued to slide down her cheeks. Max nodded. She would too, with her instinct for order, her practical stubbornness.

"Coffee first," he said, pouring water into the electric pot.

She shook her head, straightened her small body. "Dressed first."

Sweet Betsy, Max thought, watching her. At 28, with both her parents healthy, her experience with death was indirect, tenuous. Brushing her teeth, fastening her belt, she prepared for what lay ahead like a young soldier readying for duty, leaving her civilian things in their proper places.

"If Sidney's crying," he said, as he pulled a sweater over his blue jeans, "don't let them try to make her stop. If she can't cry, you got trouble."

Betsy was putting their collection of shoes, usually tossed under the bed platform, into a very straight line. He turned from her and pulled a comb through the snarls in his beard. Once it had been all red. Now, it was streaked with gray.

He'd known Shirley Pendergast twelve, fourteen years? Years longer than Betsy. In those days Shirley was a nebulous, untidy girl whose wispy hair framed a rounded forehead and cheeks still chubby with baby fat. Max remembered mostly the rather vacant look in her brown eyes. She hung out with jazz musicians; she was almost a fixture in after-hours lofts, slowly ridding herself of a healthy Midwest orange-juice and Crest toothpaste breathlessness in the long nights and cold mornings of the Lower East Side. Max talked to her once in a while at a big party: innocent, glib, trying to be hip. She'd married a black guy named White something, David White, he was a writer, or hoped to be, and for a time the two of them had a storefront place on 7th Street and ran a little magazine, splotchily printed on absorbent newsprint. Jazz reviews, poetry, political articles: "Free Martin Sostre!" "Hands off Cuba." It went sour.

A lot went sour, Max thought, fourteen years ago. The newspapers hadn't even begun to talk about The Sixties then—and now all the TV and newspapers say over and over is how The Sixties is over.

Max hadn't seen Shirley or her husband for years. But, at his first big exhibition at the Quorod Gallery, she came plunging through the crowd trilling "Max, Max, Max Birtwhistle!" and kissed him on both cheeks, hugging him with the warmth of a long-lost friend. She was almost unrecognizable. She'd become sleek and mature. Her hair and body were expensively dressed; the baby fat gone. She had, she told him, just become an associate editor at Wilson-Hill on the strength of her work on *DEEtroit Nigger*, the autobiography of a young black woman activist. The book was a mega hit, holding a place on the bestseller list for months. David was gone, she said, but they'd had a daughter who was now three years old. She invited him to dinner.

Her basic prissiness, hidden carefully during her Lower East Side days, had risen again and melded with a crust of sophistication. She'd lost once. Once was enough. She was playing the rules now. And she was charming. After she'd served the right charming dinner, they had sex because it was the right thing to do, on the white rug in front of a heavy glass coffee table with the right intellectual magazines on it, and small red coffee cups, and blown glass brandy snifters.

He hadn't wanted to talk to her afterwards. But he did. He hadn't wanted to make it with her that night, but he had. Max winced slightly. He hadn't wanted to do a lot of things.

Betsy was putting on her coat.

Maybe Betsy was another one of those things. He brusquely reminded her to take some money. She had already, and she kissed him tenderly, mistaking his withdrawn silence for grief.

"Will you be all right? Would you rather I stayed with you?" she said suddenly.

"No." He hadn't wanted to sound that short, so he patted her shoulder and made a smile: "Just call if you won't be back for supper," he said.

He pushed the cross bar police lock back into place behind her and surveyed the long loft space they shared. Shirley Pendergast fried in a fire. That's a hell of a tag line. A hell of a way to get her out of my life. Max felt ugly and pinched. After the cold intimacy of their re-meeting she'd stubbornly kept track of him. He'd loose touch with her, bump into her again; turn down her invitations; she'd show up at a friend's. He had introduced her to Robby, on the off chance she might know someone who could help him get his work published and she'd become his editor. Her company published two of Robby's densely written, obsessive novels—the first to huge acclaim, the second not so much, but publication changed Robby into Robert Rosen, noted avant-garde author.

Fire! He leaned against his storage racks and stared into his splattered painting studio. The artist's nightmare. He had a large canvas, stretched and primed, but not yet touched, not touched for weeks. Shirley had no paint soaked rags. She didn't smoke. She hardly drank more than a brief glass of white wine. She'd even become a vegetarian after making senior editor, keeping herself lean and hard for the high-pressure world of mainstream publishing.

A fist was pounding on the loft door.

"Shit," he hissed to himself. The pounding was frantic; he gave in. "AW right. COMING!"

"Thank god you're here!"

Robby Rosen leapt at Max, grabbing both his arms: "Oh, man, I'm in terrible trouble, I'm in terrible trouble." He held on as if he were in the grip of a spasm. "For godsake, lock the door!"

Max extricated himself and thumped Robby fondly on the back. "You know I always lock that door. Take it easy."

Robby was strung to the point of quivering visibly; his eyes, red-rimmed; his face, unshaven.

"Is Betsy here?" Robby's eyes moved rapidly from platform bed to Max's studio, to Betsy's unlit workshop where her pottery wheel, cans of clay and cluttered shelves stood, dusty and unoccupied. He skittered to the sunny south-end towards the sink and stove, his head thrust forward as he checked out the part hidden by the half partition. Then he sagged onto a stool at the counter, cradling his close-cropped black head with pale fingers, shaking it back and forth.

Max slipped behind the counter to light the burner under the water kettle, to make, this time successfully, hot coffee for death shock.

"I've heard," he said with his back to Robby. "Betsy's

gone to Lynn and Mitzi's. They've got Shirley's daughter to take care of."

"Heard? What have you heard?" Robby shot up bolt straight.

"Shirley Pendergast. She died last night," Max answered slowly.

"But what have you *heard*?"

"Robby, have some coffee." Max pushed a mug across the counter.

"Don't patronize me, man. I'm in danger," Robby shouted. His eyes were not just red-rimmed, they were panicked and his normally pale face was almost gray. This is too dramatic, Max thought, even for Rob.

"What's the story, man?" he said gently.

Robby's sensitive horse-face was always like a screen on which conflicting states of mind could play out like a Punch and Judy show. Right now, terror and pity were duking it out. His whiskers were two days old, almost a beard. Tears welled in his brown eyes. "It's my fault."

After a silence Max said: "Go on. Give."

"I need your help, Max. I gave Shirley something. I gotta get it back."

"It'll take a little while. You know. Her parents'll be flying in. Betsy will probably help them go through her apartment."

"It isn't there. She took it with her. Oh god, why did I give it to her?"

Max leaned across the counter. He kept himself down to two cigars a day. He took two from the box and offered one to Robby. Robby slapped it out of Max's hand, bending it against the counter, and stood up, as if to leave.

"For godsake," Max snapped. (Those cigars cost $2.50

each.) "Will you sit down and stop acting trapped. I'm your friend, meatball. Did you write her passionate love letters?"

Robby glared on the verge of a stream of invective, but Max saw fear and compliance replacing his furious glare. Robby sat back down.

"Look, Max, I can't, I mean...." He steeled himself: "I gave her a notebook and copies of some documents. I gave them to her because she didn't really believe me." His voice sped up, rising in pitch. "Even so, I thought Wilson-Hill ought to know. I thought she ought to show this stuff to them. I gave it to her Thursday morning, when I was in midtown for my class. I went back up to the country later, like an asshole. I never thought she'd leave the city! Soon as I'd done it, I knew I shouldn't have. They must be..." He broke off. He started again, lowering his voice. "I called her to get it back but she'd left the office. I just about went nuts last night, knowing I shouldn't have laid that stuff on her. No one answered at her apartment but I never dreamed she'd taken it to the country. I had to come down here to get it back from her. I didn't trust myself to drive. I took the early train. I got a cab and by the time I got to her office, the cops had called. They were all berserk. That girl who works for her, what's her name, Marsha? all I could get out of her was Shirley took a whole lot of stuff, mostly my manuscript, she said. Wanted to work on it. Work on it!" He stopped again, to master himself. "I know this all sounds weird, but there are reasons. And I just don't know what's happened. I mean, the first thing, I have to do," he said, as if giving himself directions, "is find out if the stuff is still there, since that means one thing, and keep anyone from looking at it who shouldn't. And if it isn't there," he looked urgently into Max's face, "it's really serious Max. If it isn't there I think Shirley was killed for it."

Max looked at the coal on the end of his cigar. Killed. Fire. He looked at his friend.

"Say something!" Robby said.

"I'm not sure what we can do."

"Go to her house, see if we can find it!"

"There was a fire there," Max reminded him softly. "The fire department'll have it boarded up. If it was really bad, the structure's undermined. Either way no way can you get in."

Robby began to sputter.

Max put his hand on Robby's arm. "You want me to come up to the country with you?"

Relief and guilt made war in his face. He nodded, and his face broke into its wonderfully luminous smile, the smile that almost magically squelched people's exasperation. Max knew it well but still it was irresistible. He smiled back.

"So we'll say it's the only copy of your manuscript," Max said, beginning to rehearse.

"It's not my manuscript! Weren't you listening? There's another copy of that up at Wilson's. They always keep another copy."

"Yeah," Max answered. "Let's hope the folks up at Hargate Corners don't know that. It sure sounds better than a story about mysterious documents. You want them asking you to explain?"

Robby buttoned up the coat he'd never taken off. "You're a prince, Max," was all he'd say. "You're a prince."

All the way up the Westside Highway, past the Cloisters, through the Bronx, into Westchester on the Saw Mill River Parkway, Robby retained a determined silence.

"I don't want you involved," he had repeated, twice.

He sat with lips set, a self-consciously silent hero. Max grinned to himself as the Volvo chugged stolidly along the roadway. I'm driving you, schmuck that I am, that's involved, he didn't say. And why he was doing it he didn't want to say. It was actually good to be out on the road, away from the backlash of his last show. Away from the need to analyze his disappointment and figure out his next move. Away from the empty canvas hanging reproachfully on his painting wall.

The brilliant blue morning had given way to a wan white overcast. Small crescents of blackened snow hugged the northeast corners of buildings and embankments. Early March thaws had left long heaps of dirty debris along the softened shoulders and in the swampy drainage ditch called the Saw Mill River. Grey ice was sheeted with stagnant water. An amateur oil painter couldn't make a more depressing muddy mess, Max thought. He felt another twinge. Betsy's voice had sounded very small and strained. He'd promised to be home by seven. He slowed behind a rust dotted van doing forty in the passing lane, knowing his promise was one of those good intentions doomed to be broken.

On a road map, Hargate Corners is not quite sixty miles

from New York City, marked by the tiny dot indicating "pop. 1-2,000." An octopus of highways offered dozens of routes to the northern suburbs—all of them were fouled, clogged with cars, forever under construction, flooded when it rained, beset by fender-bender accidents. Ironically, the fact that a drive to Hargate took more than two hours—except in the dead of night—protected the area from the suburban development that had eaten the placid countryside of Westchester. In the rounded mountains of Putnam County, Hargate Corners was still a backwater. Signs painted on the old buildings along the main street proclaimed original Dutch and English families as their owners: Van Wyk's Hardware, Pierce Construction Company, the DeCammert Brothers Building.

Buried in the underbrush of the thickly wooded hills, low stone walls marked off the pastures and vegetable fields of the 17th century. Shoots from tumbled apple tree hulks still struggled to renew themselves. Farming had petered out. In the 1920's, much of the land had been appropriated for watershed and reservoirs. Summer camps and rest homes for the city's sick supplanted some farms, a boomlet nipped by depression and war. The trees grew thicker and more stately. And now in the 1970s, exurban "pioneers," art-types mostly, looking for country places, were beginning to acquire and fix up ramshackle houses and barns.

As Max turned the car from the parkway to follow a narrow two-lane blacktop winding through a valley, he noted the contrast between the first two houses. The nearest, smack against the road, was roofed with rusted tin. Its wooden sides were faced with odd sections of black tar paper, fake yellow brick, and shiny greenish vinyl. In front of a sagging stable a disemboweled Chevy truck sat on its axles in the mud.

The next house stood at the end of a curving drive, almost at the summit of the hillside. A copper weather vane, set on slate shingles, spun languidly against the whitish sky. Manicured hedges hid the first floor. The top of the house was white and perfect, with large green shutters bolted shut. Max could just make out the blue plastic balloon, protecting the huge swimming pool behind it. Max knew this house. A drama critic summered there. Robby had taken him to one of the critic's famous weekend parties.

Both the buildings shared the spare lines and balanced form of pre-Revolutionary farmhouse style; neither neglect nor restoration had obscured them. Common buildings, shaped not by an individual but by a collective idea, Max thought. The grace of a faith in reason....

"Turn here, here!" Robby shouted suddenly. Max spun the car onto a narrow gravelled track.

"What the hell for?" he growled, nursing the car.

"Circle round," Robby said. "Pick up Highway 9. Don't let 'em know we're here."

"How in the hell am I gonna find out about your goddamn notebook stuff if they don't know we're here!"

Robby looked scared. "Please," he begged, "don't go by Shirley's." Then after a minute: "Oh, shit."

The detour took twenty minutes.

#

The Hargate Corners fire department was a two-story garage at the end of Main Street. One of the garage doors was open and a skinny young man with a short yellow beard was sitting on the running board of the fire engine. He didn't know nothing, he told them. Max and Robby would have to see the cops.

"Everyone's sleeping 'cept me," he told them, giving them the outlander stare as he lit a filter cigarette.

Max's stomach angrily reminded him he'd eaten nothing since last night and it was well after one. They parked across the street from the police station and jail—one barred window on the second floor—and Max dragged Robby into the drugstore grill. The cheeseburger was greasy but it was hot, the coffee pallid and mud colored. While Max gobbled, Robby sat rigid in front of a mug of lukewarm water. It was doing very little to the tea bag lying at the bottom.

A teenaged employee wiped at the empty counter, watching them. She recognized Robby. She knew he was a friend of the dead woman, the city woman. She tried to manage a solemn, sympathetic look but excitement made her pale eyes sparkle. Something really bad had happened to one of the city folks, the summer people. She wore a heavy high school ring on her right hand. It must have been her boy friend's ring for it was wadded with tape to make it stay on her thin finger. Max looked at the stern angles of her English face, the long nose and thin mouth, spare as a cut line, thinking of the two farmhouses up the road. She had disfigured herself in conformity to an alien fashion culled from magazines and TV, plastering her skin with cheap pink make-up and distorting her mouth with heavily applied dark brown lipstick.

Finally she couldn't contain herself: "You here about Miz Pendergast?" she blurted.

"He's pretty upset about it," Max managed with his mouth full as Robby jumped and almost spilled his cup. "So, does anybody know what happened?"

"Dunno. Must a been some kind of party out there last night." She leaned against the counter. Her breasts were also disfigured by a pointed disproportionally padded bra. "That's what I heard."

Max went on chewing.

"Some kind of party," she repeated.

Max looked up.

"She couldn't of been alone." The girl nodded agreement with herself.

"Who called the fire department?" Max asked.

"Oh, that was old lady Haas. But she don't even live on Horse Creek Road. She's up by Miller's. That fire was so bad she thought it was a forest fire. Sky was all pink."

The last bite filled Max's mouth like a burden of uncooked dough. He looked down the counter, focusing himself on a rack of plastic hairbrushes.

The counter girl strove to recapture his attention: "Fella I know, said Lester told him looks like someone *set* that fire."

Max tried to look mildly bored but Robby shoved his cup aside and jammed his shaking hands into the pockets of his coat.

"Lester?" Max said after managing to swallow. He took out his wallet to pay.

"Yeah, Lester. He's a volunteer. All the volunteers was out there."

Max laid the money down.

"That's pretty smart," he said admiringly. "I mean, it must be pretty hard to tell what was going on."

"Oh yeah?" said the girl scornfully. "This fella said that Lester said there was gasoline cans and beer bottles laying all around. He ain't supposed to tell!" she added triumphantly. "Musta been some kinda party." She continued confidentially now, "They got the state police in on it. I seen the cars."

"Oh yeah?" Max shook his head and clicked his tongue. "When was that?"

"Bout twelve o'clock. Just after I came on." She pocketed the quarter Max had left by his plate, looked suspiciously at Robby standing by the door. Paranoia was almost visibly around him like a large black blanket.

"They took the body to Maquaset. The state police went over there to look at it."

Robby was out the door; Max caught up with him next to the car.

"I can't go through with it. I can't go in there." He was chattering inside his coat, his shoulders were hiked up to his ears. "They've killed her. It's really true."

The counter girl was looking at them through the smudgy plate glass window. Max led Robby out of her sight line and shook him by the shoulders.

"Sit in the car. I won't be long," he ordered and strode purposefully back across the street, feeling the girl's eyes riveting his back like two red-hot needles.

Twenty-five minutes later, Robby was still slouched

in the passenger seat almost shrunken inside his coat. Max slammed the door and turned the ignition key thoughtfully. Robby hardly blinked. Max slapped his friend's leg lightly.

"Let's go to your house, man," he said. "Looks like that girl was right. Something ugly happened."

Robby's brown eyes looked woodenly at Max. He nodded, just barely.

#

Three years ago Robby had had what his psychiatrist called an "episode." Out to lunch, was what Max called it, the black dive. Louise had skipped with a young TV producer. They went to Hollywood, to fame and glitter land. In her final words to him, Louise made her reasons clear: she was through forever with Robby's moods, his poverty and self-absorption, his all-night writing binges, his erratic sexual demands, his failure above all to be, as she succinctly put it, "a man among the men." Cruelest of all, she'd taken their two-year-old son Jerome with her, "to protect him from his father's destructive influence."

After four months of schemes and scenes, of screaming long distance telephone calls, lawyers, detectives, threats and counter-threats, including Robby's crazed plan to kidnap Romey from Louise's Hollywood Hills apartment, he'd collapsed. It was Shirley, Max remembered, who had found him a place to stay up here in the country after the hospital released him. It was Shirley who had held his hand when the final court order came, forbidding him access to his child except in supervised hours, in L.A., a continent away. It was Shirley who had talked a local landlord into winterizing a little cottage so he could live there, commuting to the city three days a week to see his shrink and teach his writing classes at City University.

As he threaded up the back road to Robby's place, Max wondered how seriously he should take Robby's cold lethargy. Was this the start of another black dive?

"Robby. Robert! Snap out of it. You better tell me what this notebook business is all about. Me being in the dark is no good. The head cop in there's a nice old guy. Treem his name is. He even gave me his card so I could call him later. But they don't handle things like this. He's called the state police in. It's bad. They've ordered an autopsy and everything left in her house has been impounded. Some team of forensic specialists is due in the morning to start going over everything. Or the arson people. It'll all take time. Are you listening to me Rob? Besides everything else, there's a ton of paper work; he told me they'd have to do a complete inventory before they can release any property they've got."

That is if they don't consider the property evidence, Max didn't add. Treem, the old police chief, was geezery and pleasant, but he was nobody's fool. Max had had to answer a lot more questions than he'd been able to ask, and he hadn't liked it.

To his relief, Robby answered. The reply didn't remove Max's concern about Robby's state of mind.

"We have to buy some bread, Max. Turn around. The bakery's just outside Peekskill."

"Why the hell am I doing this?" The question racketed in Max's skull so insistently he thought he'd said it out loud. He was speeding.

"Left here" Robby said.

Max kept driving. He cornered as bidden, slid through an intersection on the yellow.

"It's the second shop. There."

"Well?" Max said.

"Go buy two loaves of pumpernickel rye. And then ask for a Challah." Robby handed him a five dollar bill.

It was a two-story frame building in a row of the same—all the storefronts facing graveled parking spaces, with small apartment windows up above. Clean paint and a neat sign announcing "Fine Bread" contrasted sharply with the boarded-up barber shop to the left and a neglected hippie second-hand store to the right. The window revealed brown paper lined bins of seeded rolls and carefully stacked loaves. Max shoved the heavy wooden door. A buzzer sounded. A beefy white-clothed figure moved lightly from the rear door into the immaculate space between mirrored wall and wooden counter. There wasn't a stray crumb on the floor.

"Yesss," the man said sharply. By his lined face he was easily in his late sixties, but his movements were athletic, and his body seemed trained and well cared for. Under the white paper hat, he had pale hair, cropped skull close. Dough over steel, Max thought, looking into the white-blue eyes. They were small, and blank, and far apart. From just under the left eye to the edge of the jowl that blurred his blunt jaw ran a long thin gray scar. The mirror reflected the back of his head, his square uncurving neck, his heavy shoulders.

Max asked for pumpernickel, sliced.

"Und?" the man asked. The smell of fresh slicing filled the room. He was slipping the loaf into a white waxed-paper bag.

"Honest bread," Max said smiling, "what a treat."

"One seventy-eight."

Max unfolded the bag end and sniffed nostalgically. "Real," he said in German. "Ah, it's such a long time."

The baker's eyes glinted suspiciously. He answered slowly at first, also in German. Yes, my bread is sound, he said. As he picked up speed, Max lost all but the jist: he'd taught himself all he knew about bread, his bakery was very clean.

Max smiled delightedly, nodding his head.

"Helmut, who is here?" The sweet bird-like voice was easier for Max to understand. Her German was more like his grandmother's. She was standing in the back room door, a tiny all-gray lady with sparkling yellow eyes. She was also swathed in a gleaming white apron but underneath it was a brown print dress. The long sleeves were rolled halfway up her softly wrinkled arms.

"Go back inside, Else. Just a customer."

"But I thought..."

"No. Go back." His face clamped shut. "Anything else?" he asked in English.

"Oh, yeah. Got Challah?"

"I can't help you."

"You know, egg bread. For shabbus." Max kept on smiling.

"No. One seventy-eight." The man's face reddened. "Who told you that?

"Juden brot," Max insisted.

"Get out! Get out my shop. I want nothing from you. Nein!" the man roared.

"Leave."

Damn, Max thought, here we go again, this same damn routine stretching all the way back to his boyhood when kids caught him singing one of his grandmother's songs. They rocked him for a Nazi bastard. He was seven. Tears in his grandmother's eyes when he told her what happened. Tears in his own when he realized he'd be tarred by every crime committed by his grandmother's countrymen if he claimed anything German as his own.

"Control yourself!" Max shouted in German. His grandmother had raised him while his parents both racked up overtime in Detroit's war work factories. "Control yourself!" was his best-remembered German phrase.

The baker looked stunned. There was a crazed look in his eyes before he turned his facial expression blank. But the red color did not diffuse.

Max fumbled for his wallet. He flashed a two-year-old Brooklyn College faculty I.D. card with the city seal and a Polaroid mug shot. "Mr. ?"

"Heppmeyer," the baker managed.

"We check up on complaints. Is anyone harassing you here?"

The baker's face went pasty. "No. No."

"We take it very seriously. If there's anything organized behind it, especially then."

"No."

"Jews in this country are very sure of themselves."

"No."

"Too sure of themselves," Max pressed. "Sometimes they think anybody with a German accent..."

The man's eyes glittered but he stayed still.

"How long have you been in business here?"

"Five years."

"And before that?"

"I was in Newburgh. I have a license. It is all in order." Heppmeyer paused. "You are not the health department."

"You have friends here?" Max continued.

No answer. Mr. Heppmeyer was getting his nerve back.

"You are from?" he asked.

"SBAS," Max said. "You have trouble with the Jews here?"

"No. No. I am a peaceful man. What SB?"

"Small Business Advisory Service," Max improvised. "We try to keep things peaceful. So decent folks can do their business."

Heppmeyer's face went crafty: "Lissen, you should check up on next door here. I myself have called the health department. Dirty windows, the snow is not put away. And their bugs. Their insects, they come in here. Go and see. Everything is peaceful here. No trouble. None. I have my papers."

"And I have my bread," Max said, tired of the charade. He pushed the bill across the counter.

"No. No charge. Just next door. You see."

"Are they Jews?"

"I am a peaceful man. Take your bread."

#

"Okay?" Max flung the bread bag on Robby's lap.

"No Challah, huh?"

The streetlights had come on, mixing their metal green shadows with the watery pink afterglow of sunset. Cold and pale but glowing, an effect Max had tried to capture in the central panel of "Extensions." Images flipped by in his head. Robby was smiling, smirking even.

"Goddamn it. Spit it out, man. Betsy's back at Broome Street waiting for me. I'm up here doin' cockamamie errands for you. It's nearly six o'clock!"

"That man's a Nazi, Max," Robby said quietly.

"Very likely. Weren't they all? It's almost thirty years."

"Max, you asked. I'm trying to tell you. It started just like you're thinking. Weren't they all. You know. Goddamn writer's imagination. But I'm so fucking thorough when I do things I started checking on him. You know. Research. I went to Immigration, looked through Wanted lists. Dossiers. It's taken months. People are very helpful to a college professor doing research, you know. I've even had his signature analyzed. Was and is, Max. I can prove it. That's not the worst of it. He's not alone here, he has friends. And they know things."

Max's back prickled. Involuntarily he checked the rear view mirror. Empty grey road, chill darkening countryside.

"Goddamn it, Robby," he protested. "How do we get to your place from here?"

"Believe me. Please. It's not fantastic. I kept telling Shirley that Wilson's lawyers oughta check out my materials. I must have told her a dozen times. My new book isn't fiction! Thirty years ago, blah, blah, blah. You think that's too long ago to matter? Too many of you people think that. Don't you read the papers? So finally I gave her all my stuff. I gave her my notebook. It's all in there, Xerox copies, photographs.

"His real name is Schmidt. He was just a junior level Gestapo bastard. Just following orders, you know the drill. Just following orders with the Dutch police in Rotterdam. You wanna hear some of the things he did?"

Max said he'd heard enough already.

"Drops out of sight in '45. Then, it's Argentina, 1946. Mexico, '47. He's just as smooth as silk. Somehow he's nowhere till he pops up in Newburgh as an immigrant from Canada eight years ago. Where'd he get the money for all that moving, Max? He sets up a fucking bakery in Peekskill of all places. And he buys the building. You know Peekskill's history, man? Ever hear of the Peekskill riots? There's a right-wing underground around here that makes the Weatherpeople look like college kids."

"Most of 'em were college kids," Max replied. "I guess that didn't stop them from doin' some deadly shit."

"Max, they killed Shirley. And they're coming after me."

Robby was crying again.

Max made coffee in Robby's filthy kitchen.

"I don't know what's got me the worst, causing Shirley's death or being scared myself." Robby had taken a shower as Max asked. He was sunk in a gut-sprung overstuffed chair, wrapped in a gaudy velour dressing gown. He was composed but very pale, his hair wet and shiny. Max chucked a pile of papers and books from a second chair and settled in with his cup. They had checked all doors and windows. They were locked in.

"I need help. Will anyone believe me?"

"I dunno." Max was wondering if *he* did. Fiction is Robby's art and life; fiction is what he lives with inside his head.

A car rumbled across the wooden bridge just below Robby's driveway. Robby scrambled to the window, peered carefully through the curtain with his body pressed against the wall.

"Johnson's truck," he said after a minute. "He's gone on past. Jesus! I can't take this. It's a nightmare."

"Look, Robby, if—and to me, I'm sorry, man—it's still if—if this Heppmayer character knows you've been checking up on him..."

"He does."

"Yeah?"

"I told him. I don't know why I did it, but I told him. I had to see his face."

"And?"

"I thought he was going to kill me."

Surprise, surprise, Max thought. Just tell any old German you run into that you know he's a Nazi. "Come on, Rob, what do you mean?"

"He came across the counter at me. I mean he was jumping like a goddamn gymnast. I could hear his old lady screaming in German all the way across the street to my car. Then the store was closed the next day. Locked tight. I thought they'd run. Three days later, he was open again. Bold. I tell you, this guy has friends."

"When was this?"

"Three weeks ago. First of March. You should have seen his reaction. He knows. And he knows my car, now, too."

Max rubbed his head thoughtfully.

"Robby, have you thought of contacting the Israelis? You know, if you're right, well they're pros at this sort of thing and they do have a thing about war criminals...."

"I did that already, man. Whatdaya think? When I thought they'd run, I went right to the goddamn whatchamacallit, legation in the city. What a slick bunch of bastards *they* are. 'We don't make a policy of interfering with the private lives of American citizens.' Blah, Blah, Blah. And they filmed me. Plus they wanted my documents all right, but I wasn't going to do *that*!"

"Why not? Why would you think they'd tell you what they'd do next anyway? You couldn't just hand it over to them and be done with it?"

"Look, I told them my sources. Well, almost all. It was plenty to start on. Oh, a guy took notes. But nothing. They were patronizing me."

"That sounds about right to me," Max said. "I mean, Robby, how would they know your motivation?"

Robby jumped again at the sound of a second car. Max joined him by the window.

"Just a car, Robby. Just a car." But Robby's emotions were building.

"That notebook is everything, Max. I'll believe I'm all wet about this just one way: if my notebook is still there, in Shirley's house. And I mean all the stuff in it intact. Anything less is just too long a chance to take. I should just wait for you to believe me? Until when? When something happens to me? You need to see my blood first? That right? Shirley's isn't enough for you?

"Robby, cool it, take it..."

Robby swung. The punch landed dead center on Max's diaphragm; breath oofed out of him and the sudden sickening pain released all the rage of a bad day.

I shouldn't do this, Max thought coldly, seeing himself recover his balance, seeing himself step in. His left arm blocked Robby's next wild swing; his right connected with a satisfying crunch against the stubble on his friend's unshaven jaw. Before he could stop himself, left, then a second right had followed, well-oiled accurate body blows. Robby's delicate unworked hands cupped around his face as he went down.

You can't travel too far, Max thought. He looked down at his hands, the paint colors ground in under the nails, the fingers bent and thickened from years of use and abuse. Shit. He used to watch his dad at the kitchen sink, trying to clean out the ground-in soil of a thousand chassis. "No assembly line for me," he said ruefully to the mute shape on the floor in front of him. Ach, Robby, there's got to be another way. Not this violence, not this stupid brute force shit. So where'd I go to be different? To art? Brute force makes art, makes pictures work. Plus I've even got a quota. Do twenty paintings every year or my contract with Quorod goes belly up. Assembly line no shit.

Mucus was running from Robby's nose and a thin thread of blood snaked from the corner of his mouth. His jaw was already bluing.

I hope to hell I didn't crack one of his teeth, Max thought, rubbing his burning knuckles. Asshole, asshole.

He cleared the couch of its burden of old clothes, books, left-over dishes, and dragged his moaning friend up onto it. He propped up the head. He folded the limp hands neatly across the chest. Robby wasn't really passed out; he was watching Max perform these actions with groggy comprehension. Max went about collecting ice, a towel, a bottle of whiskey.

No disinfectant, he noted, poking in the grubby bathroom cabinet, just three different kinds of tranquilizers. Max picked the strongest one.

Robby eyes were full of reproach, but he complied with Max's ministrations. Yes, he said, his vision was clear. Yes, he drank some water first, then swallowed the proffered pill and lay back, eyes closed, with a wet towel across his head and ice cubes wrapped in paper towels tucked against his jaw.

Max poured a whiskey for himself. Then he took his glass and the bottle to the telephone. He reversed charges and sipped, waiting for Betsy to pick up and listen to him telling an expurgated version of why he had to stay with Robby till the morning.

He didn't realize he'd fallen asleep, just sitting there. When the phone rang, he leapt for it. It felt like a bolt of lightning. It was Betsy.

"Max, Max? I didn't mean to wake you."

"Yeah. Yeah."

"Are you okay? You sound awful."

"Are *you* okay?" Betsy sounded awful too; she sounded scared.

"I'm all right. I'm...Max I feel sick. It was on the evening news. They showed her *house*—and the cops were saying they think it's arson. What the hell happened?"

"No one knows yet, honey."

"And now this guy keeps phoning our house. He says he's," she gulped, "was, he *was* Shirley's lover. His name's Dick Conway. He's called for you three times since midnight. I think he's pretty drunk. He says I've got to tell him where you are, he's got to talk to you. Do you know him?"

Max was silent.

"Max?"

"I know him," Max said, looking around the hallway. He focused. The chair Robby had propped against the front door handle had been moved. He poked his head around the corner to the dim-lit living room. The couch was empty.

"Hang a second," he said. He missed the little hall table and heard the phone receiver bang on the floor as he grabbed for the front door. Robby's Volkswagen was rolling silently down the driveway. Its lights were out. The angle was steep and Max couldn't tell how many people were inside. He could hear Betsy's tiny voice screaming frantically from the mouthpiece.

Max snatched it up: "No time, I'll call you later."

By the time he'd got his car to the bottom of the drive, Robby's car had switched its engine on and dropped from sight over the deep cut at the top of the hill. Max opened his window, kept his lights off too. He guessed Robby's old VW had a quarter mile lead, close enough for him to hear its faint put-putting in the cold quiet air.

The road curved, clear of trees. A quarter moon was low in the sky. He pushed for speed and saw it up ahead. The driving lights were on now so there were two red tail lights to follow. He was closing the gap between them when the red lights were suddenly gone. The road ran straight, a good half mile down an incline before cutting across another small bridge and disappearing. Max stopped, with his head out of the window, listening. Through the frosted weeds to his left, something flared a moment. A putt-putting, growing fainter. He backed up in the dark until he saw the two-tire mud track through the meadow. His car jerked over the ruts, stones clanging on its underside.

"Christ preserve my axle," Max said fervently. The track let out onto Route 9. A Buick with CB antennae whizzed past. "Which way, good buddy?" Max closed his eyes, trying to make map images and recollected land forms meld into a coherent pattern. Left would go to Peekskill, he decided. Hunch made him turn right.

He drove with his headlights on now, studying the

shapes of land and buildings as he went. A chicken coop fronted with recycled house window frames. Yes. And across the road, he made out a darkened diner and its stark sign: EATS. The turnoff for the road to Shirley's summer house should be at the bottom of the next steep hill. Max picked up speed and made the turn.

Horse Creek Road was bordered by thick trees and even leafless they filtered the quarter moon. He kept his headlights on. They picked up the reflecting signs, "Reservoir Preserve. No Trespassing," nailed to trees every two hundred yards. Then came a chain link fence surrounding a summer camp. Just past its wooden gate was a turnaround with a roadside picnic table. Robby's VW was parked next to the litter can. It was empty.

Max pulled in behind it. The hood was still faintly warm. He opened the driver's door, ran his hands across the seat, then checked the backseat. Only one person had been inside. Then he took the keys out of the ignition and locked it up. He walked along the poorly surfaced road to the end of the camp fence. Just opposite was a small lawn and a boxy little house where a couple of craftspeople with their little son had tried to make a go of selling ceramic pots and macramé belts on their front porch the previous summer. Their sign was still there, "Crafts by Jennie and Gerry" encircled in a garland of hand-painted daisies. The windows were shuttered. Max walked around back, listening.

An overgrown lilac hedge separated their yard from the long sloping field in front of Shirley's place. Shouts suddenly broke the silence; two flashlight beams began bouncing up and down, one from the trees on the far side of Shirley's house, the other from somewhere on this side of it. Abruptly the soiled ruin of the house appeared in glaring light. A police car spotlight was aimed directly on it. From Max's vantage point at the hedge, it was like looking at a lighted stage set.

A black jacketed state trooper was holding Robby against the partially collapsed house front. As Max watched, he pulled Robby's arms behind him and deftly snapped handcuffs on. Robby tried scrunching himself into a low squat, but he was jerked upright, spun around, shoved against the house wall, and roughly frisked.

"Norm? Norm!" the trooper hollered. A running figure in boots, blue jeans and brown jacket came into the brilliant circle of light. The state police car's inside lights went on—they were brownish yellow in contrast to the brilliant spot—and Max could see a second uniformed officer holding a speaker mike at his mouth. The blue jeaned man shoved Robby's shoulder, and leered at him. He towered over Robby, clearly firing questions that Max was too far away to hear.

He did hear Robby's high voice floating downhill; he was yelling "No, no man, no," and thrashing against his captor.

Max wedged himself into the lilacs, pressing his cheek against the branches to stave off nausea. It was shit enough, he thought, that he'd hit Robby. Now Robby was going to get it again. Max drew in a deep gulp of the cold air and began a run up the hill. The two troopers, half dragging, half carrying Robby had reached the cop car and shoved him in. Max was too late. He stopped and crouched where he was. As they pulled away, the driver spun the spotlight across meadow, sending crazy slanting shadows and illuminating a second car, this one unmarked, on the road a hundred feet beyond the driveway. The trooper blinked his headlights at it, then turned and sped down the road passing within a few yards of Max, who lay flat, his hands shoved deep in his pockets, his face in the dry grass. It was a bit of luck that he was wearing a dark grey sweater. The trooper in the unmarked car was on his own. After a few moments, Max saw a match flare inside.

Bet you're bugged, missing the fun, he thought.

He eased his way out of the watcher's line of sight and made his way back to his car. Max cursed Robby both aloud and silently the whole way to the Hargate Corners police station.

#

The little building looked deserted. The door was locked. A faint yellowish light through thick glass transom made the gold letters of "Hargate Corners Police Department" black. Max alternately pounded and pushed at the bell. He could hear it ring somewhere inside.

Nothing. He was about to give up when the door opened.

"Can't do nothing for you. I'm alone here." The man wore a sprung and shiny dark blue uniform. He looked more like a retired postman than a cop. He'd been asleep. He was easily twelve to fifteen years older than the elderly chief, Treem, Max had spoken to that afternoon and he was in no mood to stand in the cold on his tired legs. That business out on Horse Creek Road was none of his concern.

"That's not township." He stepped back to shut the door.

"Hey, wait. Do you know where they'd take him? My friend, Mr. Rosen?"

"Not him, who?"

Max's head buzzed; the man was beginning to shut the door again. Max stuck his foot in it.

"Don't do that," the policeman reproached. He looked a little frightened.

"Where would they take him," Max repeated firmly and slowly the way he'd speak to someone deaf or sick or very drunk.

"What's your name? You've got no right to come in here."

For a crazy minute, Max thought he was going to threaten to call the cops. "The state police picked up my friend on Horse Creek Road. Where did they take him," he insisted, trying to keep his tone patient.

"Why didn't you say so. Maquaset." He stepped back from the door and unsnapped his worn black holster. "You take that foot out of my door or I blow a hole in it." He pulled his service revolver out and, wavering slightly, clicked the safety off and pointed it at Max's leg.

Max removed his foot and stood quite still. The policeman kicked the open door so it shut heavily in Max's face.

Max walked up the dark main street, away from his car, knowing the hit of terror would pass out of the ends of his fingers and toes if he concentrated on a reasonable breathing pattern. After the first long block he allowed himself to lengthen his stride. All the store windows were dark and shuttered. A few had a work light on in the back. A blue neon farm insurance sign blipped and hissed. It was mended in two places with black tape. Another painted sign read "Anderson's Grocery (Lennart Anderson, Jr., prop.)" The covered porch reached to the curb. Max took the two steps up in one and clumped across the wooden planking. Three plastic-covered newspaper dispensers stood by the door at the corner. They were all empty. The porch continued around the side of the building. There wasn't much else to Hargate Corners.

Max shoved his cold hands into his pockets. About 300 yards down the road stood a low barracks-like building; the small square windows were painted red and lights were on inside. Several cars and pick-up trucks were drawn up beside it. Max walked faster. Please don't be a church, he said to himself. He could hear a TV set as he neared the building and saw the pink electric sign: Bar & Grill. The door had a latch handle.

"Closing in ten minutes," the bartender said. He wore a red and black plaid hunter's cap.

"Bourbon double. Glad I made it." Max smiled and laid five dollars down. "What's the best way to Maquaset? I'm parked down Main Street."

He got a quick set of directions. "Should take you about fifteen minutes this time of night," the bartender added.

A black and white Western movie flickered on the TV. None of the patrons were watching. Five men in conversation clustered where the bar made a rounded corner to the wall. The bartender stood by Max, watchfully. He pushed a soiled ashtray toward him as soon as Max pulled his cigar pack from his pocket. The only other customer was a man at a table by the door. He had his feet on the chair opposite and seemed to be asleep. The group was animated. Their voices had been loud and opinionated when Max opened the door but they'd looked up as he entered, dropped their volume, and shifted positions on their stools. Now the noise level rose again. Max looked in his glass and asked if he had time for another.

"Ah, sure, no hurry," said the bartender, delivering it. He moved down the duckboards to the group: "Hey, Sharkey, Dave, you guys, gotta close in twenty minutes. Stock up."

The ashtray represented a naked blonde with red-tipped breasts and open mouth. The ash bowl occupied her belly and the lip for resting a burning cigarette was her vagina. Max broke his burned match between his fingers and put it in his pocket.

"It is not, ask Len!" The youngest of the men was gesturing, pointing vaguely toward the ceiling. He was wearing a dark jean jacket decorated with biker patches. "Old man Howard was his uncle. She musta bought that place the week he died. That was three, four years ago."

An older man with a bill cap agreed: "Just like I said, just like I said." The others weren't listening to him.

A sandy-haired heavyset man with a deeply creased neck leaned across the older man and prodded the stomach of the younger man sitting on the other side of him. He had a soft baby-like belly, timid eyes, and round cheeks. He was wearing a purple satin basketball jacket with a high school patch on the back.

"Whatta *you* think ole Conrad? You ain't been saying much. You missed your chance with her yuh know. She really gave you the eye last summer."

"Oh, Sharkey," the kid answered, half hurt.

"Oh yeah," Sharkey continued, "I remember. 'Oh please Mista Hilberry, mow my field, oh please Mista Hillberry, get me a cord of wood.' Missed your chance to mow *her* field, she sure asked you to."

The plump kid tried to evade the jabbing finger. "Jesus Christ!" he exploded.

Sharkey left off, gulped from his mug of beer, then glared coldly at his victim over the rim of the mug.

"Oh, you know how he t-t-t-talks," the fifth man interceded. He was slender and bucktoothed, with large hands and a quiet face. He gave the kid a kind of squint, long familiar to all of them. We all know Sharkey's a pain in the butt, his eyes said. He was wearing unlaundered white coveralls with a name embroidered over the left front pocket in dark blue thread. "Lay off C...C..Conrad, 'kay, Sharkey?"

"Anyway, how come you got so rilled up when she was in your office?" the older one called Dave chimed in.

"When was that?"

"I sent her in to talk to you. Sounded to me like a good job of work."

"You mean that swimmin' pool bull shit?" Sharkey shook his head as if the last ounce of patience he possessed had to be called on. "Lissen, Dave." He shook his finger. "I'd like to learn you but there are some things you just can't teach. When a broad like that comes prancing in, you just know you got nothin' but trouble. She don't know what she wants."

"Seemed pretty clear to me. Those prefab pools are mostly fool-proof. A day with the dozer. I figgered you'd get a real good price outa her."

"Dave," Sharkey said, nodding with bitter wisdom, "the day a job for a bitch like that is fool-proof is when pigs fly. Even that day she changed her mind a dozen times. I mean look. She buys that broken down old shack, Len's crazy uncle built it when he was so stupid old he wet his pants, place don't have a decent crapper in it, don't have one wall that meets the other full and square, and what does she want? Swimmin' pool, the place got a have a swimmin' pool for that nigger brat of hers."

"It ain't right to talk like that," the old man said.

"Shut up, Ben."

"Whatever she was, she's passed on now."

"Don't change the fact. Bein' dead don't change a whore into an angel."

"Just the same, seems like your mouth runs," Ben said.

"I wonder if they're gonna find who did it?" Young Conrad had finished his beer. He pushed the glass back across the bar and released a thundering belch. "Donna's... real upset. So's my mom. They think it's addicts come up from Peekskill."

"Sharkey, you ready t-t-to go yet?" The man in white coveralls asked. He had tucked a cigarette behind his ear, and was ignoring his companions.

Max swallowed the last of his bourbon. He could have used another, and he knew he ought to have some food. A bitter taste overpowered the artificial whiskey warm and curled down his innards like a long black worm.

MAQUASET

It took more that fifteen minutes to find his way;
Maquaset was all the way on the other side of the
county—and more time that that to find the headquarters
of the state police—a utilitarian yellow brick building
on a sloping lawn above the highway to Connecticut.
A huge cast-concrete New York State seal was the only
relief on its squat shape. Last year's dead grass was tinted
cosmetic pink by the crime-stopper lights that studded
the grounds. Max looked at the motto on the seal as he
walked up the tidy gravel path. "Excelsior." You bet, Max
thought. Where's my goddamn shining sword?

Max was shuffled from desk to desk; he waited as told.
The third wait was longest, the third chair, the hardest.
His tired mind began to entertain itself. A slide lecture
on Memling's "Stations of the Cross" flashed in his
head as vividly as if he were still on a hard chair fifteen
years ago while a lecturer droned on and slides clicked
in a darkened room: close-up, detail. 'Station Three—
and now you'll notice how the artist has distorted the
dimensions, the typical method of handling proportions'
... flash, click, 'Station Four—now the artist, makes the
figures larger to bring us...'

Max rubbed his eyes and got an adrenalin rush as a
uniformed trooper beckoned, "This way fella."

He was to see an officer of the SBI, he was told. The
initials interpreted themselves the way a puzzle will
suddenly become plain: State Bureau of Investigation. He
was ushered into a private room.

The beige walls were scuffed and marked where chairs and feet had rubbed against them. The green linoleum tiles were pitted with old cigarette burns. A grey metal desk was piled with papers; the green leatherette swivel chair stood empty. The room's only occupant was standing by a coffee urn on a stand gritty with spilled sugar and stacked with white plastic cups, both fresh and used. He looked up briefly. His white-flecked blue-black hair was cut mod style and luxuriant sideburns framed a Roman nose so monumental the rest of his face was almost swallowed up.

"You wanna cup of this?"

"I do," Max said. "I take it straight. Thanks."

The man was in a kind of costume: a leisure suit with metalized threads woven into its pattern, a bright white shirt with a wide open collar, a chunky gold-plated necklace, a matching pinky ring, Italian-style black leather shoes with built-up heels. A more expensive version of this getup belonged to self-styled high livers, the big spenders, the gaudy suburban businessmen who speed in their oversized cars and like to intimate that their business deals are only quasi-legal. But this man's eyes were watery and tired, the eyes of an overworked bureaucrat, and the heavy pinky ring only emphasized a fragile almost womanish quality of his pale hands.

"You gonna need this, Irelli?" The officer who had led Max in, stood at the door holding a large reel-to-reel tape recorder.

Irelli handed Max his coffee and concentrated on loading his own cup with four big spoonfuls of powdered imitation cream.

"You want this?" the officer repeated.

"Sir, I don't have a statement that's any good to you," Max suggested.

"You want this plugged in?" the man at the door persisted.

"My friend is very upset. That's the size of it."

Irelli settled himself heavily behind the desk; he looked piercingly at Max's swollen knuckles letting him know he'd noted them; he looked into Max's eyes. Max felt his ears burning as if he were twelve years old. He held his eyes steady.

"Well, yeah, I coulda been a better diplomat."

"His face looks pretty bad, fella."

"Look, he's real upset. Ms. Pendergast was his editor. She did a lot for him."

"Did he sleep with her?"

"That's not what this is all about."

"What is this all about?"

"She was working on his manuscript, a new book."

"He has keys to her house. That looks pretty friendly." Irelli sucked at his hot coffee.

"Yes, they were friends. He's taking it hard. Besides which he may have lost a year's work in the fire. He just wasn't thinking very clearly."

"So answer me, did he sleep with her?"

"I don't think so. What I mean is, they might have had a short thing a couple of years ago. It's beside the point. They were colleagues."

The officer with the tape machine was setting it up. His big Adam's apple worked up and down as he listened. His hands were chapped and red. He couldn't have been more than twenty-three and he looked a little overcharged, excited, like a kid at the circus. He set the mike on the desk, flipped the button on. Then he squatted to watch the volume needle, and spoke quietly into the mike.

"Friday, March 20," he checked his watch. "Twelve fifty-two a.m., Detective Vance Irelli, SBI, interrogating. Present, Officer Henry Schuyler."

"State your name," the young man said sharply.

"Max Birtwhistle."

"Oh, Hank, for chrissake." Irelli shoved the mike aside. But he didn't switch it off.

"This fellow Rosen, is he under psychiatric care?"

Max considered for a minute. "I believe he sees a doctor in the city, about once a month."

"He gave his last address as Rockland State."

Max sighed wearily. "He had a mild breakdown a couple of years ago. I don't think he was in there more than three weeks. Look, remand him in my custody, can you? I'll post a bond. Whatever you want. I'll be responsible for him. You want to talk to his doctor? You want to talk to the people at Wilson-Hill? That's his publisher. Robby is excitable but he's not crazy. He's a writer. He may have lost a whole year's work if his manuscript was burned up in that fire."

Irelli looked stonily at Max.

I hope the hell he hasn't been carrying on about Heppmayer. The thought teased Max's gut. He mustered a professional tone. "Are you planning to charge him with anything?"

"Trespassing at the scene of a crime?"

The answer was a question, or more properly, a dare.

Do you want me to say something stronger? the tone implied.

"When can I see him?"

"You a lawyer?"

"When can his lawyer see him?"

"Soon as he gets here. You have something to tell me, fella. When you gonna?"

Max set his cup on the desk edge and got up.

"You're not doing your friend any good, you know."

Max turned to leave.

"Hold on. You better give me your address and something to corroborate it." Max pulled out his wallet and slapped it on the desk.

"Hold on there," Schuyler said, half-rising. "One-sixty-two and one-half Broome Street. What's this one-half?"

"Downstairs is a fabric jobber; he's 162."

"College professor, I see," Irelli remarked, leafing idly through Max's wallet, squinting at cards and pictures.

"Used to teach."

"Unemployed?"

"No," Max said.

"Well, where do you work?" Irelli was looking at a snap of Max and Betsy, both very tan, in tattered shorts and skimpy tee shirts, standing on the deck of a white sailboat.

"Well, there, in the summer." Max pointed at the picture. "I do some teaching at the Rockhill Colony in Maine. I'm a painter. An artist," he explained, seeing the quizzical look. "Do you need all this?"

"I need you to tell me what you know about the Pendergast fire."

"Yeah? Okay. A woman is dead. A little kid is orphaned. You people found gas cans in the driveway. And if I knew more I'd tell you. Do something for me now: tell my friend Rosen I'll be back this morning with the best damn lawyer I can hire."

The stairs felt steeper than usual. A muffled whisk slap, whisk slap, got louder as Max reached the door. He clicked all three locks.

Betsy looked up, breaking rhythm. She was wedging clay. There were lavender circles underneath her eyes and the ghosts of last summer's freckles stood out on her pale nose and cheeks. She slapped at the red-brown loaf on her plaster wedging board.

"It's too young," she said. "It doesn't feel right."

He came up behind her, kissed her ear. Which tasted of clay dust.

"And it's full of bubbles." She cut the loaf on the wire to show him."You been up all night?"

"Seemed the best thing to do."

"Don't be sore."

"Was Shirley rich?" she asked.

"Don't be sore."

She turned to look at him, half wary. Trust won. She leaned against him and put her arms up under his. He felt her warmth through the layers of their clothes.

"Robby's in a stupid jam. He's in the slammer." She looked up, eyes widening.

"Does Shirley have a lot of money?" she asked again.

"Why?"

"This guy Dick, he was rambling about money on the phone. And saying stuff about Shirley's brother. He called Lynn and Mitzi and said Tyrone might come there and they mustn't let him in.... Robby?" What he'd said had finally dawned on her. "What did he do?"

"Something dumb," Max answered.

"Oh Max, they don't think Robby!..."

"I dunno. I gotta see if Wilson's will do something. He needs a lawyer."

"*You* don't think Robby?"

"No. Absolutely."

"You need some sleep," she said. She climbed out of her crusty coveralls, holding one of his hands as she pulled her feet free, graceful as a Watteau lady. Underneath, she was wearing blue jeans and a sweatshirt.

"I'll be all right," Max said. "I could use breakfast."

"Was Shirley murdered?"

Max sat at the counter watching Betsy move...icebox to coffee grinder, frying pan to water kettle...he didn't want food. He wanted her. He shook himself. There'd be no way to keep himself awake afterward. Damn it.

"Was she? Dick says she was."

"You must have talked to him a lot."

"I told you, he called three times. Each time he was crazier than the last. He was in a real rage because I wouldn't tell him where you were. You said you know him?"

"He's a stockbroker. He likes to hang out at Spring Street. He's into art." Max sighed.

Dick Conway's flushed face, his expensive three-piece suit, his long body hanging at the crowded bar, buying drinks for the newly in fashion, yeah he was a regular weekend sight. Looking for the deals that held promise. The attention he'd get. Money and art, they circle like a bad love affair.

"He buys a painting once in a while, or makes trades for stock tips. He tried it once with me. I ended up giving him advice." Max laughed. "Now he thinks I'm a wizard."

Little boy fool, Max thought.

"He went with Shirley?"

"I saw them together. About three weeks ago." In fact, that was the last time he'd seen Shirley, he realized. Shirley had been wearing a mink hat. It was in the afternoon. He'd gone to the bar to meet a former student; the place was quiet; and he'd been surprised to see her sitting in a booth, since it was office hours. She was grave, intimate, maybe even worried, Max recalled, leaning toward her companion opposite. She'd flashed a look of recognition and then deliberately turned her head meaning don't break in. He'd recognized Dick by his broad jock shoulders and the small round, carefully combed-over bald spot. Dick hadn't turned.

"So what did he say?" Max asked.

Betsy straightened over the frying pan, trying to put events in order. She ticked them off on her fingers: "Tyrone Pendergast is very dangerous and I mustn't let him in. . ."

"I didn't know she had a brother."

Betsy touched her next finger: "Lynn and Mitzi mustn't let him in. He might try to kidnap Siddy." She raised her eyebrows at Max, and touched her next finger: "We mustn't believe anything her lawyer says; he's a shyster."

"Did he give his name?"

"Starkazi, I think. Something like that." She held her fourth finger and smiled a little: "You're the only person who can be relied on. You're the only one who can straighten this thing out." She dropped the fingers and poured the rest out in a rush: "They were going to get married, he said, but no one should know. So why did he tell me? He'd made an awful lot of money for her on something to do with drugstores, I think. . .or was it drugs. Max, would Shirley get herself mixed up in drugs? He said she'd pulled in more than a quarter of a million dollars, and he mumbled on and on about short term and long term and I didn't know what he was talking about. Then he called me a stupid cunt and said didn't I realize that Shirley had been murdered. Damn!" She slipped the singed ham from the frying pan to his plate, slapped the eggs in, and slammed the toaster lever down. A little domestic violence calmed her.

"Well?' she said, wiping her hands on a towel.

"Did he leave you a number?"

"God, three of them. Home, office, and some Wall Street bar." She'd taped slips of paper to the icebox door. She pulled them off and handed them to Max.

"I'd like to push the phone right down his throat."

"He was drunk."

"Okay."

"You've never heard of Tyrone?"

"NO."

"Mitzi has. She says Shirley was afraid of him. Oh Christ, it's quarter of." She gulped at her coffee and gave Max his eggs and toast. "Lynn's going to the airport to pick up Shirley's folks. I promised."

"You haven't had any sleep." Max chomped the toast angrily.

"You haven't either." She tipped her head up at him.

"Don't you teach tonight?" he managed with his mouth full.

"It was last night, dummy. This is Friday. I cancelled anyway. Oh Max," she said, bundling herself in her coat, "it's rotten over there. Siddy spent all yesterday afternoon crouched up on the top bunk. We took turns sitting up there with her. The other kids are scared so they're acting up like beasts. Know what she keeps saying? 'Shirley told me I could have a swimming pool.'"

Max dunked his head in a sink full of cold water, then stuck dishes in the sink and changed his shirt. He set the slips with Dick's numbers on the shelf by the phone and dialed Wilson-Hill.

"No one," he was told crisply, "was expected in editorial till nine thirty."

There were two Starkazi's in the phone book. One said residence on West 86th Street; the other was a business on Third Avenue, midtown by the number. He dialed that one. "Personal business," he explained to a secretary, "A matter possibly connected to one of Mr. Starkazi's clients." After a wait, he was connected.

A roughened elderly voice confirmed that Ms. Pendergast was his client. He'd learned of her death this morning in the *Times*.

"Has a Tryone Pendergast been in touch with you?" Max asked.

"Are you representing Mr. Pendergast?"

"No," he said.

The voice was cold and guarded. "What can I do for you?"

"Shirley's parents are due in about an hour," Max said evenly. "Should they be in touch with you?"

"Please. I'd appreciate your asking them to call me."

"I'm sorry," said Max. "Did you say you handled her personal or her business matters?"

"I didn't," the lawyer answered. "I'm not at liberty to discuss this on the phone. I'm sure you understand. My condolences to you."

"Yeah. Thanks. And mine to you. You don't know where I can reach Tyrone, do you? It's important."

"Mr. Birtwhistle, I'll see that anything addressed to him in care of my office is forwarded to his home. That's all. But he'd hardly be there now," he added in a slightly friendlier tone. "I'm sure he'll want to join his parents for his sister's funeral services."

"I understand your position, but that won't help me," Max said.

"I'd prefer to spare the senior Pendergasts a problem they just don't need," Starkazi said frostily.

#

Max dialed the public library reference room: Mike Cowber was a poet and smart and sweet and Max had been a friend of his for years. He asked him to check Starkazi in the Bar Association directory. He lit a cigar to wait with.

"Less' see, Max." He could hear Mike rustling pages, and echoes from the marble dome of the central reading room. "He's sixty-three; a two-A rating, CCNY, Fordham Law. Seems to have taken him a rather long time to get through school. Bet he went at night. Was a partner in Kolodi, Ives, Starkazi, dissolved 1958; senior partner Starkazi and Fisher since 1960. What do you want to know?"

"Can you tell what kind of law he does?"

"Real estate, mostly, personal estate, trusts. That's what it looks like. Why you want to know?"

"Just want to find out if his nose is clean. Shirley Pendergast was his client."

"What a lousy thing," Mike said after a pause. "Shit. Well, the Bar Association thinks he's straight. You know. Doesn't look like a ball of fire though. What a goddamn thing," he repeated.

"Yeah."

"Listen, is there gonna be some kind of service? I'd sorta, you know."

"I'll let you know. And thanks."

"Doin' my job. Don't forget."

"No, I won't."

#

The morning rush was over. The subway train looked like the site of an abandoned demonstration. Newspapers lay in trampled shreds across the floor, along with empty coffee cups and shards of food. Unintelligible, angry slogans in spray paint and marking pen were scrawled over walls, windows, seats, and doors. The car's only other occupant glanced guardedly at Max, tightened her crossed legs and her grip on the plastic department-store shopping bag she held on her lap. Her hair had been bleached almost white and teased into a balloon-like shape. Shiny with lacquer, it could be a spun-glass football helmet, Max decided. She bent over the open shopping bag where the head of a small dog protruded. Because she knew she was being observed, she fondled the dog's ears and began to speak to it in chirruping undertones. The train, unweighted by its usual burden of bodies, rattled harshly. The dog had a pink bow on its head. It was trembling.

Max got out two stops later to make his way toward the glossy glass and plastic tower that housed Wilson-Hill Publishing and its subsidiaries. The receptionist on the 23rd floor was nervous. She was a slender, young, self-consciously proper Puerto Rican in a tailored gray wool dress. She tapped her rose-painted fingernails against the side of the console phone while relaying Max's request to the office of the editor-in-chief.

"I'm very sorry," she said coolly, her eyes skirting Max's head and roaming across the wood panels and bookcases of the reception room, "Mr. Hammer is not in yet. He's... they... there's been..."

"I know about it," Max said.

Her face broke from its posed correctness and she looked up at him with warm worried eyes. "You one a hah writers?"

Max shook his head. "A friend of one of her writers."

"He hadda go up there to identify ha body. People been callin like crazy. Think Miss Jennings could help you?"

The whiff of Brooklyn Spanglish coloring her speech was put away as she made her second call. Just the same, she was not at all sure how to act. Her secretarial training clearly warred with her desire to ask questions and share in the surge of bewilderment, shock, and sadness. The blinking telephone called her back to her uptown role as Marcia Jennings opened a paneled door and padded across the thick carpet toward Max.

Marcia's tanned, well-educated face was puffy and reddened; she wore silver wire rimmed glasses and carried herself confidently. She was about twenty-four. Her clothing had an arty cast: a bright Mexican sweater, a chunky silver medallion, a dark skirt, knee-high low-heeled boots.

"Let's talk in my office," she said giving him an icy hand to shake. "We're all pretty upset around here."

She led him down a long white hall from which offices of various sizes opened off. Most doors were open and the decors ranged from minimalist austerity to graduate student slobbery. She led him into a small suite. This one was all business. Piles of manuscripts in neat boxes and folders, a wire bin of galley proofs, cups of sharpened pencils. A poster of Sun Valley was scotch-taped to one wall and above the desk a framed photograph of people in bright ski clothes smiled down. The inner door to Shirley's office just beyond was half ajar.

Marcia set herself firmly in her seat, but as Max made preliminary small talk she edged about, first sticking one booted foot underneath her thigh, then switching legs, and, finally, yanking both feet back to the floor while she rummaged violently in the back of her desk drawer. She came up with a battered pack of menthol cigarettes.

"I've been trying to give up," she apologized, offering the pack to Max after extracting one for herself, "but, God, now, all of this." She lit up, and blinked rapidly. "To tell you the truth, I still can't...I keep expecting to see her coming down the hall. I, I..." She puffed rapidly with shallow breaths.

"They should give you a few days off," Max said.

"I know but... but there's a lot to do. People keep calling. She had so many projects..."

"I really shouldn't bother you. I should talk to Mr. Hammer."

"I can't understand why Bobby tried to break into her house."

"He was worried about some materials he gave her."

"You mean just recently?"

"Sometime on Tuesday."

"Oh God." She stumped out her cigarette and took herself into the inner office. Max could hear her on the phone.

"...so we have more troubles, now. Tell Mr. Hammer to buzz me as soon as he gets in. Oh, God, I know!" she ended emphatically.

"Is this what you're talking about?" Marcia returned holding a dark green ledger. The edges of photographs and xeroxed legal papers bulged from its sides. It was held shut with two fat rubber bands. She handed it over.

"It's been here all the time?" Max didn't need to look inside to be sure. Notes and telephone numbers in Robby's tiny hand were scribbled on the white rectangle on the ledger cover.

Marcia blushed under her tan. "I was supposed to talk it over with Mr. Hammer last Wednesday. I just never had, oh you know." She waved her hand at the stacks on her shelves. "God. Is it important? I mean Shirley seemed to think it was some kind of nuisance. She was *humoring* him."

Everybody humored him, Max thought, removing the rubber bands. He leafed through the book. It was a knotted jumble demanding concentrated unpacking. Like Robby's novels, he thought. Robby had given it to Shirley, here, on Tuesday. There was no way Heppmayer/Schmidt, or whoever he was, could have connected Shirley to the man who had confronted him in his bakery three weeks ago. No way. Dear, cracked Robby. The real Schmidt would be canny, he'd have thirty years experience in laying low. Surely he would run to protect himself if he sensed a real danger. But Heppmayer hadn't run. Max put the rubber bands back carefully.

"This should go in the vault, Marcia. At least till Robby's out of this damn mess."

"Is it that important?" Marcia goggled behind her elegant glasses.

"Oh, I don't think so, but it would upset Robby if it got lost."

"That's for sure." She grinned a little. She put the ledger into a large clasp envelope on which she printed: Please Hold for Robert Rosen. "I wish he'd told me what he was looking for. He really freaked me out yesterday. But then..." Her buzzer rang. Hammer, Max thought. But it wasn't. Marcia hunched over the phone.

"No," she said urgently. "No, she can't. Tina, damnit, tell her I'm in a conference, that's what receptionists are supposed to do...oh Tina, no," she wailed, looking at Max with put-on exasperation. "Don't talk to her while you have me on the line!" Her put-on expression became the genuine thing. She slammed the phone down and went for her door. Max stood up behind her.

A tall coffee-colored woman was striding down the hall; behind her the young receptionist was pleading ineffectually, "Please! Miss Burke! Please come back."

A thin balding man with a potbelly like a little watermelon emerged from his cubicle. The woman shoved him with two hands against the corridor wall. His mouth made a soundless circle of astonishment.

"I know her office here," the woman announced hoarsely. "Where Shirley secretary? You her?"

"I'm her assistant," Marcia stressed acidly, "and I'm in a meeting just now. I suggest that you..."

"You damn right you in a meetin. You meetin me." She moved past Marcia and confronted Max. "An I doan need company."

"Don't bully me, lady." Max looked into her eyes.

She decided to ignore him.

"I'm Charlene Burke," she announced to Marcia. "You people got a manuscript that belong to me. I want it back." Her even features worked steadily, smoothly, like the drive shaft of a tanker. Marcia fluttered, trying to restore the world she understood, a world where people stood in line when asked, where people feared embarrassment, and dreaded above almost anything else being considered rude.

"Miss Burke, please understand, nothing's going to happen to any papers that belong to you. We'll be happy to send them back any time you ask. That's all you have to do."

"Well."

"But I can't give them to you this minute."

"Don't give me double talking, girl." Burke shifted her weight forward, brushing Max's shoulder as she leaned over Marcia. The office was little more than cubicle and was a tight fit for three people. Max backed slightly, ready to grab her arm if she took a swing.

"It's in the vault." Marcia's voice was both shrill and placating. "Mr. Hammer isn't in yet...I'll be glad to send it to you. I...we'll send a *messenger.*"

"I don't much care how you do it but I ain't leaving till I git it." Charlene was on firm ground. Her ability to overpower had been proved two times in just the last two minutes. She took her ease sitting down in Marcia's desk chair and adjusting the folds of her thick gray cape.

"I'll see if someone else can sign." Marcia fled.

The whole floor seemed to know of the upset. There was shuffling and buzzing along the corridor. Max could hear doors open and close, a man's voice yelling until a door closed on the sound, then more shuffling. Charlene Burke sat like a rock.

Max took the chair he'd had before, the visitor chair beside the desk. The neck of Charlene's cloak was edged with black ostrich feathers that stirred from her rather rapid breathing. Her head was elongated by an intricate wrap of brightly patterned African cloth. She'd worn this same headgear on a TV talk show Max had seen as she cooed maternally over poems by ghetto school kids.

"Were you a friend of David White?" Max asked.

"Huh?"

"David White. He and Shirley used to be married."

"Don't know no David White," she said.

"They used to run a little magazine together. *Tide Turning,* something like that. About ten, twelve years ago?"

"Never heard of it."

"Then you and Shirley must have met later."

"We met here," Charlene answered. "Look, I got no business with you."

"You might have. I'm looking into Shirley's death."

The Brooklyn College card wouldn't get him to first base with Charlene, but he reached for his wallet just to see what effect making such a move might have on her. Her hand flashed out to stop his arm.

"Look man, get it straight: I met Shirley here, I saw her here. Thass it."

"You seem anxious about a manuscript. Have you been having trouble with her?"

Charlene tightened her lips and stared at his face.

"If you've been having trouble, you should tell me before I hear it from them. Is this a new book?"

Charlene shook her head.

"It's not a new book?"

"It's the same book, man. I don't have to tell you nothin. Just you *try* harassing me..."

"*I* didn't come charging in here pushing young girls around," Max pointed out mildly. "What's it all about?"

"I got no trouble with Shirley. Look, man, I'm real sorry she died like that...." Her eyes softened for a second and for just that long Max wondered if she were sorry. Is anyone at home underneath all those clichés? It was hard to connect this caricature of belligerence with the passionate delicate voice that cried out from the pages of her book. Maybe that Charlene only exists in the book, he thought.

"You no cop." She was eyeing him shrewdly. "What you tryin to pull?"

"I work for a fire insurance firm."

"Fucker." She was still nervous.

"The police are working on a homicide theory."

She pulled her cape tightly across her knees. For protection this time, not as a gesture of royalty.

"What's this all about?" Max persisted.

"About nothin," Charlene mumbled. "You heard that lady. I got a right to get my book back anytime I ask."

"Miss Burke, how good to see you again." The voice was male and booming, greasy with professional charm. It belonged to a stocky, florid man, whose slightly shifty face was topped by a thatch of perfectly barbered gray hair. He was holding a thick gray box. Marcia stood behind him. Her ears and cheeks were very pink.

"Russell Burbage," he said, sticking out his hand. "Sales Vice President. Surely you remember." Charlene extended a limp hand. "I'm terribly sorry to hear you were upset. Of course we all are. This is a terrible loss. Miss Pendergast was one of Wilson-Hill's brightest lights. We'll never replace her."

She looked at him heavily, then focused on the box he held. "I jus want what's mine."

"Why of course you do." His tone was almost that of a psychiatric nurse. "*Anytime* you wish to claim it." He set the box on the desk. "I know it's a bit early in the day, but if you'd like to step into my office, perhaps I can offer you a little something. These are trying days. Trying days," he repeated.

Charlene flipped efficiently through the pages. "This ain't my book!"

"Miss Burke!" Burbage protested.

Burbage looked around. Max was a nonentity; Burbage

looked through him. "Miss Jennings," he summoned, tossing the noose on Marcia's neck, "apparently there should be another copy here."

"I don't understand," Marcia quavered.

"I want *my book* back," Charlene thundered.

"That's the original copy Mr. Burbage."

"Don't try to con *me*, girl. I'll break your face."

"Miss Burke, Miss Jennings. This will never do."

Marcia was about the cry. "Please, Mr. Burbage, this is the original manuscript. The one the typesetters worked from was. . ."

"Miss Jennings, give his woman her property, on the p.d.q."

"But we're not supposed to. Don't you *understand?* I'm sorry, I didn't mean that. Shirley told me Mr. Hammer says it's just the policy, we're supposed to keep all the editing in our files, it's...I never...Please, Mr. Burbage, the only other copy is the *edited* manuscript, the one the typesetters worked from. That one's not her property!" And she did cry, that is large tears rolled out of her eyes and caught where her eyeglass rims rested on her cheeks.

Burbage turned from his inability to control the scene and, for the first time, registered on Max sitting by the desk. "Who are you? What are you doing here?"

"Max Birtwhistle," Max said, rising from his chair, extending hand, smile, and formal manner.

"This here is the trouble," Charlene said to Max triumphantly. "This jive bunch'll say 'oh yes Miss Burke, oh any lil thing you want Miss Burke' then turn they mouth inside out, right while you looking at 'em. I don't know nothin about who fried Shirley but if you on the track of trouble, whyn't you look right here."

"Get that file, now." Burbage snapped his fingers at Marcia. "Birdwhipple, would you mind, sir, I think it would be best, ah, for you to wait in the reception room. To your left it is. We have a minor misunderstanding here. Our staff is under quite a bit of strain."

"You stay right there," Charlene commanded. "I don't mind a bit having the inspector see the way you people do things here."

"Miss Burke, this will be smoothed out momentarily. I'm sure you understand the less experienced employees. . . Inspector?" He registered on Max again, with quite a different manner.

"It's a calling, not a title. And it's Birt*whistle.*"

Marcia returned to the door with two accordion files. She had dried her eyes and summoned a reserve of dignity. "This is everything but the page proofs. I think they're stored somewhere downstairs. But I'll need a memo to Mr. Hammer to explain this, with a copy to put in each of these folders."

Burbage gave her a withering look. She continued. She had rehearsed her speech: "I can't give them to you until I have your memos. I'm responsible. Miss Burke? Would you look in the left-hand top drawer of my desk? There's a pile of memo forms."

Charlene moved slowly, enjoying herself. She handed a form and a pen to Burbage. If Marcia's face gets any stiffer, it'll crack, Max thought, nevertheless admiring her display of sand. Everything paused while the memos were being scrawled.

It could have been an exchange at the Brandenburg Gate. Everything but heels clicking. Memos to Marcia, who pulled out the carbons and placed one in each file folder. All the other papers were pulled out and spread on the desk for his perusal. The counting and inspection took place in silence. Charlene selected a large, very battered manuscript, thick with blue pencil marks and typed additions pasted onto the sides of pages. She nodded her satisfaction. Marcia wedged past Burbage into Shirley's office and returned to present a large envelope and a two-handled shopping bag. Charlene bundled her new possessions inside, rose, regal once again, glared at them equally, but as she walked through the door, she turned to Max.

"His name's not White, it's Rashid Ujusiri. He dropped honkey wife and honkey name."

"Do you know where he is?"

"I saw him two years ago in Venice, California. I ain't seen him since." She swung her butt a little in farewell as she made her way to the exit.

"I'll see you in my office later, young lady," Burbage said, and walked rapidly in the opposite direction.

Heads were popping out of doors almost as if an all-clear bell had sounded. In a minute, Marcia's office would fill with colleagues, eager to get the scoop on the scandal. Max shut the door.

"Does this thing lock?"

"No one comes in without knocking," Marcia said. "Unwritten rule." She leaned against the wall, clenching and unclenching her fists against her skirt. She looked wild; her eyes flit across the objects in the office looking some something to vent on. "I'm going to quit," she growled.

Someone tapped on the door behind her.

"I'm in a meeting," she trilled, falsely sweet and high.

"I'm going to quit, I'm going to quit before they fire me. I'm walking out right now!" She looked at Max for argument.

"I'm in the dark," he said reasonably. "What was that all about?"

She flung herself into her chair with the recklessness of a young athlete. "Shit!" She pounded the desk with one fist and then the other. She was working herself into a state of hysterics. Max wished that he knew her well enough to put his hands across the needle sharp line of her shoulders. She was a nice kid and she'd taken the brunt from two professional bullies. At a time like this, words are second best.

"On balance, Burbage gets Bully of the Month award," he said, tapping the ends of his fingers together judiciously, "but it's a close decision."

Marcia looked up, an almost-smile twisting her face. "You don't know the half of it. Hammer will have my hide for giving that manuscript away."

"You nailed Burbage for it pretty good."

"Sales," she said contemptuously. "They don't have the slightest idea what we do up here. They think we're a nuisance. They actually think we're a luxury. Where do they think the books they sell come from? They don't think, they don't want to know. Burbage is the worst, so he's the top dog over there. That's how it works."

Max didn't want her to cry again. "What's the problem with Charlene Burke? What was that all about?"

Marcia gulped. "God. It's actually funny. That book came out before I worked here, oh maybe six years ago. Shirley told me it was an object lesson to her. She was just a little more than I am then. Oh, I guess she already had projects of her own to edit, but she wasn't into acquisitions ... that's the big time, acquisitions." She fumbled for another contraband cigarette. "I'm gonna smoke like a chimney today. I can feel it. God." Her face was relaxing a little. "I'm not exactly sure how Shirley ran into her originally. Shirley had a lot of friends in the black community. From when she was married. Anyway, that manuscript drove her absolutely crazy. The story was fantastic. It was terrifying, and real, but it wasn't a book. Charlene's nearly illiterate. She can't write a simple sentence, white or black English. What she had was pretentious and inarticulate both, can you imagine? Shirley said it almost broke her heart. So she took it home and rewrote nearly every line. *DEEtroit Nigger* was Shirley's book. Jesus.

"The thing was then she had to convince Charlene that she really hadn't changed it that much. That was harder work than the rewrite. She managed somehow, used every guile she could think of. And the book hit it all, you know? Prizes, bestseller list, and there were foreign rights to over twenty countries, paperback sales.... Have you ever read it?"

"It's a beautiful book."

"It made Shirley. She got a huge promotion and freedom to develop her own list. You know, bring in writers of her choice. But you see, it made Charlene too. It created 'Charlene Burke.' Everyone wanted her for something—lecture tours, articles, TV. She was Shirley's Frankenstein. They were both sort of trapped. I guess it was awful. Shirley had to keep tabs on Charlene, write her speeches and articles. She felt guilty. She was responsible. God knows what Charlene felt about it. I think she began to believe she'd really written the book, but then what?"

"That's quite an act to keep going. Did they fight about it?"

"I don't know. Shirley was incredibly clever but almost immediately there were different political groups vying for Charlene's support. I know Shirley liked some of the people in the Rainbow Party. Oh she'd say they were softheaded drips but some of them were old friends of hers. I'm sure she was upset when Charlene broke with them. The people she got in with were very hostile black supremacy types. By the time I got here, she and Charlene made a point of meeting only here. When you think about it, it's really kind of scary. Did they get Charlene believing she'd been used? What does she think really?" Marcia's eyes widened and her young face looked a little stunned.

It damn well is scary, Max thought. It's dynamite. No wonder Charlene was so hot to have that manuscript back.

"Shirley managed to finesse it somehow. I think someone black ghost-writes for Charlene now. Since I've been here she's stopped coming around. They've talked on the phone though. I know that."

"Can I have the number?"

Marcia's fingers ran swiftly through her circular rolodex. "I only have her service and her agent. Shirley has the private line."

Sunlight poured into Marcia's cubicle as she pushed back the door to the inner office. It was three or four times larger, with a thick brown carpet and three visitor chairs. But except for a splashy child's abstract, labeled Sid with a backward "S", the room was barren as a nun's cell; everything was business. Marcia gave him Charlene's private number.

"Shirley wasn't scared about it," Marcia said thoughtfully.

"What, I'm sorry, scared of what?"

"The situation, you know, with Charlene. But she said she'd never do a thing like that again. I think she was jealous."

"Jealous?"

"I know it's queer but once she said she'd write a book herself but she didn't have the guts. Well..." She looked around the room and sadness bowed her young back.

"I have to see Mr. Hammer but could you have lunch with me after?" Max said.

"Thanks but I don't think so. I'm going home."

"Not quitting?"

"Not quitting." She gave him a tired grin. "Just done in. God. All of a sudden I think I could sleep a solid week."

Max spent a long time with Mr. Hammer's secretary. He gave her nearly all the details of Robby's incarceration; Detective Irelli's telephone number, his own. He waited. He could hear men's voices behind the heavy wooden door. When it opened at last, Burbage, scarlet-faced, almost waddled as he left, and Charles Hammer ushered Max inside. Hammer's face was drooping like a weary beagle's.

"Of course, this is all we need," he said.

Max kept it brief: "I've given all the details to your secretary. If you can get a lawyer up there to get Rosen clear, I won't take any more of your time."

"I'm afraid the situation's worsened." Hammer paused, running his hands through his thinning hair. "The medical examiner's made a preliminary report. Shirley was badly beaten before the fire. And a local taxi driver has made some very damaging statements about Rosen's behavior early Thursday morning. He was quite out of control."

"Do you know Robert Rosen?" Max demanded.

"I've met him several times."

"Robby Rosen couldn't murder a cockroach. For godsake, man, he depended on Shirley."

"Nevertheless, under the circumstances, I don't think it's appropriate for our firm's attorneys to become involved in this. I'm sorry. I'd recommend you find a skilled criminal lawyer for him."

"Robby hasn't got resources like that. Can't you..."

Hammer was fingering a glass egg paperweight and avoiding Max's eyes.

"I see how it looks but that's not how it is. And I think you know it," Max said.

"I'm sorry."

"You need a stronger word." But Max resisted the impulse to slam the door as he walked out.

#

Max sat in the back corner booth of a White Rose Bar on Second Avenue watching the beer in his glass go flat. It hadn't done a thing for the red ache in his head. Robby was no longer a literary darling. Max didn't need a stronger illustration of that. And it hadn't taken long: one highly acclaimed novel, one "disappointing" second novel, and there he was. In just a few short years—out on the end of the plank, with sharks roiling the water below, and "I'm so sorry," from the ship's captain. Hard work not to be bitter, isn't it.

He pulled out a notebook and his thick black pen from his jacket and watched himself draw grids on the smooth white page. He labeled them: Shirley, Sidney, David White (Rashid), Robert, Marcia, Charlene, Dick. Then he scratched out Shirley. Then he scratched out all the others and went to the bartender for five dollars worth of change for the pay phone.

After four referrals he got the Putnam County Legal Aid Society.

"A lawyer will be appointed when Rosen is arraigned."

"When will that be?"

The phone went dead, cut off.

He called the state police in Putnam and was told to call the Putnam county jail. He did. After a long wait he was told Robby was "under investigation," he had not been charged; as to what was planned, the voice on the phone suggested Max read the newspapers.

Max got more change from the bartender.

Information had a listing for R. Ujasiri in Venice, California. That call took a lot of quarters. Ujasiri turned out to be someone with a poor command of English. Max apologized. Next he learned Starkazi's office had heard from Shirley's parents and a meeting was set for later today. They had not heard anything from Tyrone.

Max dialed Peter Hamlin, a sculptor who also had a contract with Quorods. Hamlin's sister was a civil rights lawyer but he couldn't remember her married name. No one was home. He decided not to call Betsy. There was no way to get a message through to Robby to at least let him know that his documents were stowed in a safe in New York City, unseen by anyone up in Putnam County. Final phone call: Dick Conway was in his Wall Street office. They arranged to meet at the Broome Street bar at four o'clock.

Max ate a bowl of soup and decided to walk. What the hell.

The sign over Broome Street's window said "Henry's Mashed Potatoes" in frontier style print. The window was frosted. The name dated from the late sixties when every place that wanted to look arty had to have a campy name. The frosted glass dated from a few years later when the Soho tourist blitz began in earnest and busloads of Long Island matrons poured through the streets to visit galleries and see artists in their natural habitat.

"If they wanna come in for a beer, I'll serve em," Martin the owner growled, "but I'll be damned if I'll put up with 'em standing in gangs and pointing through the window."

So the window was covered over. But, business being business, some red-checked tablecloths were installed, and an over-priced luncheon menu was posted in a box outside the door. "Soho Quiche" "Starving Artist Salad—just 160 delicious calories" and so on. To the great relief of the regulars, it never worked. Beery stench and raucous laughter still permeated the premises. The suburb ladies opted for the Country Crafts and Kitchen Store, the Jasmine Tea, and the like, but the stink and noise had the opposite effect on weekend adventure seekers—teeny boppers from the Bronx, the Island matrons' college student children, and young office sophisticates. Were they all cruising for dope and easy sex? For sure the neighborhood changes brought an assortment of sharks and suppliers who understood how to take advantage of various available things in the volatile Soho social mix. And so the haven was invaded. "Henry's Mashed Potatoes" was "authentic" and so listed in guidebooks. Martin had got a Belgian shepherd, a baseball bat, and made no secret of the pistol clipped underneath the cash register.

It was a tribute to persistence that, in spite of all, the character of the place was still dominated by the regulars—who never called it anything but Broome Street, or even more simply, "the bar."

There must be twenty thousand bars in New York City, Max thought, as he pushed open the finger-worn door, but say I'll meet you in the bar to anyone I know and they'll turn up here.

It was only 3:30. Daytime lights were on and the place was reasonably bright. To the right, for almost forty feet, ran a massive mahogany bar battered and scarred with cigarette burns. On the dark wall opposite, over the thicket of chairs and tables, was Martin's collection of paintings. Whether these reflected Martin's taste or bad bar debts, Max had never found out. Gilson was there, represented by a lovely small collage; Herman's stark grey canvas holding three poised light grey lines, an out-of-focus landscape by a well-known photo-realist; a dreadful drawing of herself as a half-devoured skeleton by Wenton Niles. The painting that annoyed Max most was nearly seven feet long. It showed a cocktail party at Quorods. It had been done from a photograph but the bodies were flattened, painted in the palette of color television, and executed in a cynical style that denied the humanity of everyone portrayed. The painter himself, green faced and balding, smiled in a corner. Max was shown in three-quarter view, his greying hair in the pony tail he'd worn three years ago, hulking over a hideously caricatured Betsy, with skirt so short it showed her crotch and a dissatisfied whine on her face.

There was nothing to be done about it. Maybe it was Martin's way of getting back at them, the people who were his living at the price of being witness to them at their worst. Martin heard all of it: the pileup of debts, the can't-work blues, the self-pity, the broken love affairs, the fights between rivals. Max slumped on a stool and asked Gino for a bourbon straight.

Pulaski and Sikes were down the bar arguing about the President's character and motives. A woman with a don't-speak-to-me look nursed a beer at the table nearest the door, and Caroline the Virgin Queen in her signature black apron gently, lazily swept the floor around the tables. Otherwise the place was vacant, unless the high-walled booths in back were occupied. People sometimes sat there in the daytime to read newspapers or address invitations. Robby often used the one right by the kitchen to correct his students' papers or to proofread the book reviews he did for the *Village Voice*.

"Wanna drink Caroline?" Max asked.

She leaned her broom against the bar and accepted the gin over ice Gino poured without asking.

She had earned her name. She was the ice-mountain of the fairy tales, the one the knights all tried to climb without success. And how they'd tried. Under her apron she wore a leather skirt just over the knees and sheer purple stockings over her beautiful legs. Her hair hung brown, glossy and ruler straight to the middle of her back and her face was tough, sad, and sweet by turns.

One day, for her own reasons, she had told Max about the quadriplegic in the veterans' hospital she had married three weeks before he was shipped to fight in Nam. There was a farm near Utica where they could live if the doctors could only get him straightened out enough to release him. Just another operation, another round of therapy, and then.... They'd been strung out on medical promises for years. Still, this time perhaps, the doctors would pull it off. So she waited. And drank a bit too much, and kept to herself. Max never spilled her story; it had been told to him with that understood.

"You got some troubles," Caroline said.

"I do."

"It goes that way."

"A friend of mine, at least a woman I knew—she was murdered Wednesday night."

"Shit."

"Another friend of mine is in the can. They seem to think he did it."

"Sure he didn't?" It was gentle. Almost not a question.

"Yeah, I'm sure. I've spent all day trying to get a lawyer for him. I've completely struck out and I feel like an ass."

"Free lawyer?"

"As free as can be. He could borrow some money; I could borrow some money. You know."

"Have they charged him with it? I mean can they?"

Max looked into her face and thought: arson murder has got to be the hardest charge to prove. No witnesses, no fingerprints. Unless they could tie Robby into buying the gas, they couldn't really have much. A taxi driver Robby was rude to? He smiled.

"You're an angel, Caroline."

"You wanna be sure the cops know someone knows they have him."

"Well, they know I know he's there."

She finished her gin and took her broom again: "How bout Georgia Phipps? She's Peter Hamlin's sister, you know her."

"Only of her and I couldn't think of her name."

On the phone Georgia said they had met, at her brother's last opening. "You were a little tipsy," she pointed out. But more to the point, lawyer fashion, she asked piercing questions, rapid fire. Max liked her style; she thought fast, checking his information from different directions. Then she said a classmate of hers was living in Putnam County and could do a favor. She promised to call him right away. Max should understand Robby's midnight trip to Shirley's house was a bit of a problem. Trespassing. Interfering with an investigation. Still her friend could see to it that Robby was either arraigned or released. Worst case from what she could figure, Robby might be fined but he should be let go after a hearing Monday morning.

Max was still on the pay phone when he saw Dick Conway walk into the bar. He waved and went on listening. His gut was tightening. Person or persons unknown, as they say, had murdered Shirley Pendergast. Someone brutal enough to beat a woman unconsciousness and burn a house down around her. Beer cans, gas cans, a ruined building, a ruined body. Someone had done these things, someone walking around, or sleeping somewhere, or thinking about supper. Someone scared? righteous? mindless? Someone psychopathic? Or someone with a purpose? Someone would have to care about these questions. Someone would have to find out who it is.

He thanked Georgia and hung up the phone.

Dick Conway was a wreck. He reeked of aftershave underneath which came the heated smell of an all-day hangover. His hair was combed carefully over his bald patch, his vest buttoned neatly over the stomach he kept hard at an expensive health club. His hand shook slightly as he lifted his vodka and tonic. There was a dab of powder on a shaving nick below his left nostril.

"I don't know where to begin," he said.

"Let's sit in back," Max suggested. He was thinking Dick might begin by apologizing for the wild way he'd spoken to Betsy Thursday night. He turned this feeling around in his mind several times until it cooled and changed.

"This is pretty rough..." Max said. "You know, I guess, that she was murdered?"

Dick looked up: "It's definite?"

"She was beaten before the fire started."

Dick sat silent. "We were gonna get married," he finally said. "She shouldn't have waited. If we'd been married. . . I wanted her to marry me in December." His eyes were receding.

"December?"

"Coulda saved us a shit load of money. Taxes," he said in response to Max's puzzled frown. He straightened the watch on his wrist, pulled at his necktie.

Max was thinking beer cans, gas cans. Addicts from Peekskill or anywhere else, wouldn't have come to rob equipped to do arson. Not unless they'd been paid. He looked at Dick.

"Shirley kept awfully quiet about that."

"We were gonna get married. She, ah, had one or two problems."

"What were they?"

"For Chrissake, Max, don't get cute with me. I'm in pieces over this."

Max cut him off: "I get it that you wanted to marry Shirley. But she wasn't so sure?"

Dick's eyes filled with the fat tears a person cries for himself. "She'd have done it, she'd have done it. Now look what's happened!" He wiped at his eyes with the sides of his forefingers.

"Where you going with all this, Dick?" Max was sharp and cold. "Did Shirley go up to the country to be with someone else?"

Dick pulled himself together. "No," he said, convinced and solid. "No. She had to work. You know what she was like when she had work to do." He pointed his finger at Max like a boy playing gunfight. "It's her brother."

"You said some pretty bizarre things about that brother."

"I did?"

"You called Betsy, Thursday night. Don't you remember?"

"I, I wasn't very rational Thursday night."

"No, you weren't."

"Tyrone is, Tyrone's a nut case. I've had experience in these things. I know what I'm saying. But oh no, she'd say, he's my very own little brother. It's a very straight-laced family, very religious, and there were just the two kids. So Shirley made it her role to protect him, to defend him from their parents. She did everything she could to help him get out from under their thumb. Know what I mean? She was wracked with guilt when she left home without him. Soon as she could she started sending him money so he could escape. That's how it started—and it never stopped.

Shirley was always supposed to bail him out, straighten him out, fix his shit. He'd tell her really stupid stories, and she'd believe him. He told her he was planning to be a biologist, she should help him with tuition. So he went someplace on the coast of Washington to play flute for killer whales. It's not funny. He was serious. Sit on a rock and play flute for the fucking fish. Then he needed money to join some commune in Colorado. That was going to straighten him out. Then he was a 'Renaissance musician.' He and his band were going to live on barter and fuck the capitalist system. Capitalist system! I've never seen anyone more aware of the dollar than that creep. It's all he really thinks about, no matter what he says."

"Has Shirley been supporting him?"

"Not exactly. He has a small vet pension. Ten percent disability, I think. Ya know the army takes these borderline nuts, trains them, makes them really dangerous!" He was digressing, fuming, talking to himself.

"Tyrone has special training?" Max interrupted.

"Demolition. I guess everything there is to know. And since that time, with all these cults he goes in for, I don't know what else he knows. Plus he's always working out.

Look, I'm in good shape but I don't think I could take him."

"Are you saying what I think you're saying?"

Dick blushed. "I don't know. I keep trying to put it together, but I don't know. Why would he hurt her? A year ago, she bought him a farm in West Virginia. He was going to be all right if he could live close to nature. He'd left the commune. And he'd married a woman crazier than he is. They sold the farm about two months later, never paid her back. I know Shirl was furious. She promised me she'd never give in again. But he's been back at it. Around Christmas time he and his wife told her they're opening some kind of school. And last month or so he's really had the pressure on her. Max, I'm scared of him. I mean he knows damn well if she and I married he could kiss his soft-touch sister bye-bye."

"I'd never have figured Shirley for a soft touch."

"No. That's the hell of it. I don't think anyone could get to her like Tyrone. Not even Siddy. I was afraid she was beginning to crumble this January. For the first time in her life she had her hands on money. Real money. It wasn't just a question of letting him have a thou or two. He wanted fifty thousand dollars for this so-called school and he knew she had it."

"She made that kind of money?"

"I got her in on something really good. We made out like bandits. What a goddamn waste."

"Where is Tyrone? Do you know?"

"He's living in Baltimore but they have a van. They've been coming up here unannounced whenever Shirley didn't expect them. Very clever. It's like psychological warfare, y'know. The last time I know of was a week ago last Wednesday. Shirley was damn upset. I tried to convince her to get a court order to restrain him. I felt it was that serious. I just don't know. I wouldn't put anything past him. I tried to warn those dippy lesbians who are taking care of Siddy but I couldn't get them to understand. They seem to be just as scared of one man as they are of another."

"With them too, you could have been more, ah, what was your term, rational?"

Dick looked surprised and a bit insulted. He prided himself on being rational.

"The cops ought to check into this you know. Do you want me to tell them about this?"

"Yeah sure," he said, suddenly wise and cynical. "Like they're gonna do something. Max, do you know how many crimes there are in New York every day? You can't expect much from them."

"Maybe."

Max waved gently and Caroline brought them refills. Dick watched her walk away from the table.

"What a piece," he said.

I must be getting old, Max thought, tired or something. The liquid movement of Caroline's legs, yes lovely. The sweet thought of them wrapped around his neck perhaps, or...his mind wandered...but to translate it into that routine dumb assertion of male randiness...I'm as tired of male insecurity as I am of female, he thought angrily, and realized he'd been shaking his head. Dick looked puzzled.

"If I talk to the cops about Tyrone they're gonna want to know about you," Max said, bringing them both back to the subject. The bar was noisier now; it was after five and the first wave of drinkers was beginning to collect. The Friday night build up. People waiting for friends or strangers, waiting to skim a weekend's worth of release, scheming to insure themselves against possible rejections, scuffling to be in on whatever might be 'what's happening.' The bar was beginning to fill with all of it. I *am* getting old, Max thought. In a few hours, the voices would be louder. Someone had turned on the jukebox and a jazz group sobbed 'I'm here - I'm here' as if speaking for all the people assembling who want to be recognized, want to be respected, want to be with me and without me. Somewhere in Maquaset, what had been Shirley Pendergast only this past Wednesday was lying in a stainless steel icebox. She was without.

"Where were you Wednesday night?" Max said.

"Max, this is silly."

"I wish it were. Tell me where you were."

"Can you sit there and ask..."

"For the cops and for me. I just know what I'm told. I don't know what I think yet. Just like you."

"You're a weird man, you know that?"

"Tell me where you went, Dick."

"Starting?"

"Start at five."

Tears filled Dick's eyes again, this time they seemed genuine. "We talked on the phone Wednesday morning... we'd planned to have supper Thursday night, see the Danish ballet.... Wednesdays I'm at the gym by five. I did some weights. I played handball with friends, Wall Street friends. I took a shower. I ate dinner by myself, at home.

I wanted to see the play-off. I had a few bucks on it."

"You didn't go out?"

"I was home all night."

"Did anyone see you? Did you call anyone?"

"I called Lincoln Center—to see about changing the tickets. That was early though, maybe 7:30."

"Anyone else?"

"No."

"No one in the building?"

"No. The hall was empty when I dumped my garbage. But there's a security guard in the building. He'd know I wasn't out."

"Do you sign out? Does he keep a log?"

"No, not for tenants. Guests have to sign, or anyone else coming in."

"Maxela, my darling! I've been wanting to talk to you." A chubby hand slid around Max's neck. "You've been so secretive these past few weeks. Got those show's-over blues?"

It was Juan Larengiera, Don Juan, some times Juan Carlos, and behind him, as ever, skinny, silken-haired, and smiling foolishly, his friend the Dummy. Without being asked, he sat next to Max, who slid over to make room for Juan's ample bottom. The Dummy stood by, giggling softly until Dick made room for him. Juan dispensed with introductions, waving his arm; he knew that Dick was not an artist, nor, like him, a critic of art; he knew Dick wasn't gay or one of the super-rich. That exhausted the possibilities that interested him and Dick might as well have been made of glass. He turned Max's face toward him and patted his beard lightly.

"You look seedy, friend. You're drinking bourbon again."

"You can't reform a peasant, Juan."

Juan sighed with exaggerated resignation and called out in his booming voice an order for Perrier water (the Dummy never drank spirits) and for himself, a Marguerita, and a bourbon double for Max. Dick was neglected intentionally. As Juan saw it, Dick could leave now.

"Add another vodka tonic," Max said. It was done. He drained the lee water from the bottom of his glass and handed it to Caroline. "This is a wake, Juan," he explained.

"I thought it was the third degree," Dick said sullenly.

"That too. I forgot to ask you about your car."

Juan's eyes briskly searched both faces. All of a sudden he was interested in Dick Conway.

"I think you're the coldest man I ever met." Dick's face was reddening. "My car was in the garage all night. The attendant there does keep a log. Don't you care how I feel, man? Are you that out of touch?"

Max reached across the table, put his hand on Dick's arm.

"I figure it's best if I know what I'm into. I am gonna talk to the cops about Tyrone. It's the oddest damn thing I've ever done, but I'm gonna talk to them about everything I know—and I don't want the rug pulled out from under me. You probably don't know—they're trying to pin this thing on Robby Rosen. A huge waste of time. Meanwhile, someone out there did it. And none of us know why. Think about it."

Dick gulped at his drink. Little beads of perspiration popped out on his forehead.

"You're too fast for me. I keep havin'—to tell myself she's really dead." His tongue was thickening. "I need another drink...."

"An artist is the most ruthless person in the world," Juan Carlos was beginning a speech: "One is taught sentimental myths about the sensitivity of an artist, but when the sensitivity—and it is genuine and agonizing sensitivity—is matched by this incredible intention to re-order the universe, to take upon oneself the task of competition with what can only be described as the *entire* cosmos, that person—that rare person—is an artist, and is, and must be, the most ruthless of human beings. He will step in anywhere, he will—"

"Will you shut up, for chrissake. If I were ruthless, I'd pull the pants right off you and kick your butt for the twerpy review you wrote on my last show," Max blurted.

"Ahh, now we have it, now we have the real true business, eh Max? Death, nothing; murder, probable, revenge, always. By the way, dear heart, who have we been discussing?"

"Shirley Pendergast."

"Pendergast, Pendergast, I never met her—but wasn't she Rosen's editor? Are you absolutely sure he didn't do it? Every writer would like to kill at least one editor. I believe you share an identical fantasy vis a vis critics on whom you depend so much. Right, dear? It's almost a classic sado-masochistic relationship, isn't it—minus the physical delights.Strictly your puritanical choice, Maxela."

"Will you stop being so fucking glib," Max began.

Juan Carlos waved his hands: "When you stop being so defensive."

"God," Dick said into his drink. "What am I gonna do?" He banged at the table suddenly shaking the liquids in all the glasses.

"You're gonna tell me what you know," Max leaned across the table toward him. Noise, cigarette smoke, and music surged around them. Max could smell steaks cooking, and the bar's home fries. Caroline had been joined by the evening staff and was threading her way through the tables by the bar. Their last round had been delivered by someone else.

"She was worried about Siddy," Dick mumbled, "Wouldn't listen to me. That lawyer who set up the trust for her's senile or some kind of shyster. Never heard modern money manglment, tried to tell her."

"Was she scared of anyone besides Tyrone?"

A slender woman with a tropical tan and round pink-tinted eyeglasses big as saucers appeared at their table.

"Mr. Larengiera? Mr. Larengiera?" She extended her hand.

"How could dis happen to me, Max?" Dick slurred. Another drink would turn him belligerent, send him on a crying jag, or whack him out completely. There was no point in trying to stop him, Max thought. Dick waved a $20 bill. "Round f'everyone, round's on me. I'm the biggest balless wonder, I le ma fiancé get murdered. Ever hear of murder?" he demanded of the bewildered waitress. "Not like on television. Really happened to m'girl."

The woman with the tropical tan paid no attention to

this; she twinkled at Juan Carlos, equally at the Dummy, and reminded them both that they'd met at somebody's terrific party. She was wearing $85 blue jeans and a silk designer's shirt, under which the nipples of her flat breasts stood at attention. They looked like a pair of dried chick peas, Max thought.

"I heard the most amazing story about you," she crooned coquettishly to Juan. "Someone told me you're the son of Piet Mondrian. Fantastic."

"Ahhh," Juan Carlos raised his drink in a toast. "It's a wise child, you know." The Dummy giggled and Max felt Juan extend his leg to put his foot against his companion's.

"But that's fantastic. Did you actually know him? I believe he died in 1944. You'd have been a tiny child then."

"My dear lady, I was never tiny. However, I was a terrible disappointment to him. Round, you know, round. He couldn't bear it."

Max began to laugh. I must be getting drunk too, he realized. I must want to. How do you put up with him? Betsy had once asked. Max looked at Juan's peony cheeks, his wickedly teasing eyes. I must like him, he decided, and for damn sure I am drunk. He'd told Betsy: I didn't invent the art world, I have to make my way with what's here.

"For godsake, Marian, I thought I'd lost you." A tall young man in a yellow suede jacket joined her breathlessly. He was also wearing pink tinted glasses. His were aviator style, with slender silver frames. She put her cheek against his and kissed the air.

"Oh George, don't be peevish. I want you to meet Juan Carlos the critic, you know." She shoved him a little. He was supposed to make an impression but he wasn't sure how. He cleared his throat. "George just had the most marvelous little exhibition," she began for him, "tell him George. The most incredible enameled figures. He created an entire little world, houses, people, vegetation, like nothing you could dream of. The whole thing fits on a table fourteen inches wide. It took him three years to finish. Were you able to see it?"

"Poor Mondrian," Max butted in. "Didn't like round. Didn't like flesh. However did your mother get him into bed with her?"

"My mother has money, dear. Isn't that gross? Gold just rolls in off the Pampas." Juan Carlos fingered the lapels of his black velvet coat. He had a blue farmer's bandanna knotted loosely around his neck.

"I'd like to go to Argentina," the Dummy said unexpectedly. His voice was flutey and surprisingly clear.

"Does that explain everything?" Max prodded, grinning broadly.

"Oh my," said the woman, trying to retrieve their attention. "You're Max Birtwhistle, aren't you? I'm Marian Crandall. I was so impressed with your last show."

The air went out of Max's fun balloon. He turned toward Dick, now mumbling to himself in the corner. "Thanks," he managed.

"It wasn't good, you know." Juan looked up at her. His eyes weren't teasing any more. "Max is in danger of becoming a hack."

"Oh!" The woman backed off a step, frightened. George took her arm.

"Marian, please, the Dawson's are up front. They're dying for dinner. They're waiting." She let him steer her away. Max heard her say, "He's terribly rude, you know, everybody says so."

"I've got to pour him in a cab." Max jerked his thumb at Dick and squished his hip against Juan's bulky thigh.

"He'll keep. Best thing for him. I want you to eat dinner with us and come to Mother Vivian's loft. Preston's group is doing a performance tonight; I think it's going to be intriguing."

"Mother Vivian's," the Dummy echoed. This was an amazing lot of conversation from him.

"I've got too much on my mind. And you want to start on me."

Juan was well over two hundred pounds but Max managed to slide him a little way across the bench in the booth. He gave in, stood up, and waved Max out. When Max had got to his feet he put his hand on the fat man's shoulder.

"Robby's in the can. I haven't seen Betsy in days. I'm angry, and I'm tired."

"And you do know what I'm talking about," Juan Carlos said.

"Come on fella, ooze on old man." Max coached Conway. He and the Dummy helped Dick clamber clumsily out of the booth. He leaned against the Dummy's side as Max looked around for his raincoat. It was hopeless. Huge mounds of clothing were now hanging on all the clothes hooks and Max was glad he'd kept his jacket on. Dick can afford the loss, he decided grimly. Juan Carlos opened his mouth. Before he could

properly begin Max planted what he hoped was a beatific
kiss on Juan's smooth pink, delicately scented forehead,
and propelled Dick toward the door through the knots of
people and past assorted greetings. He returned them all
with resolutely pleasant nods.

Meeting Tyrone

The cool air, the dark sky, the change in noise level were all shocking. Dick buckled and leaned.

"Take it easy," Max said. He massaged the back of Dick's neck. "Don't breath too deep, you'll be okay."

He thought if they walked toward Broadway there'd be a better chance for a cab but he whirled abruptly when he saw one going in the opposite direction and Dick almost lost his balance. It was empty. Max hailed it with an earsplitting doorman's whistle. He put his arm across Dick's back and under his arm to help him across the cobblestones, slick with truck drippings and spillage. A couple stepped around the corner, heading for the Broome Street's door.

"My god, it's him!" Dick tried first to point and then clutched heavily at Max's jacket to right himself as his feet began sliding out from under him.

"There he is, over there!" the young woman shouted. She was pointing back. Behind him, Max heard a car's wheels screech. It honked angrily, passing the stopped cab on the wrong side. Dick tried to pull in the opposite direction but Max was able, floundering for both of them, to keep them both on their feet and heading toward the cab.

"What are you, Abbott and Costello?" the cabbie snarled out his window.

"It's him, it's Tyrone," Dick yelped, getting free of Max and supporting himself on the cab's hood. Max opened the passenger door.

A wiry young man had dashed across the street; he snatched Dick upright, his knees were bent and his left shoulder went down as he steadied his prey with his right arm.

"Hit em Ty, hit em," the woman screamed. She had run also across the street and was standing under the street light, clenched like a coiled spring. She had dirty blonde hair. Even in the discoloring light, Max could see her teeth were irregular and diseased. She had large, beautifully shaped pale eyes. Max stepped heavily on Tyrone's left toe, wedged his shoulders between the two men, and pushed Dick into the cab's open door.

"Mother fucker," Tyrone grunted. He tried to knee Max from behind. The cabby, unable to leave because Dick's body was still partly outside the door, blew his horn violently and then tried climbing past his meter to the door on his right-hand side. Max whirled, elbow up, head down. Tyrone moved as if to swing his right. Instead, Max butted, shifting his weight as he moved, connecting beautifully.

"Eeeerunk," Tyrone grunted. His legs flickered back five or six quick steps but not quickly enough for him to catch his balance. He skidded on his ass in the middle of the street, turned the fall into a roll, and then recovered like a tumbler.

The cabby gave up his hopeless try for the other door and resumed horn blowing, bellowing curses and threats.

"Max, he'll kill you. He's already killed his sister." Dick's voice was thin, almost soprano.

Tyrone was coming back. His body was crouched; his blinkless eyes fastened on Max. Max was concentrating.

And he was loosing his chance to retreat into the cab as Dick had managed to do. He understood this when it was all too late. The cab door slammed, Dick Conway yelled from inside, "Let's goooo," and the cabbie made a jackrabbit start sending his cab roaring and clanking down the uneven street.

"You let him get away," the woman wailed.

Tyrone feinted right, almost grabbed Max's left as he ducked, hooked a leg, out to trip him, and got a hard punch in just under Max's right armpit before Max could get his arm up, to block it. He felt the fingertips of that hand go numb. Tyrone was smaller than Max, and lighter. He was also at least ten years younger and eight drinks soberer. His eyes were exactly the same shape and color as Shirley's but his were bottomless and empty, holes drilled into the crazed beyond. An embroidered headband kept his lank brown hair out of his face. His second punch got Max in the liver, the third, as he ducked, grazed his temple and ear, and the fourth, with a sickening slam, broke against his kidney. His vision clouded and the symbols on the headband danced hypnotically. Indian devices—the corn woman, thunder, the rainbow, the Beauty Way of the Navaho.

Max was backed against a wall. He wasn't thinking at all well. This man was not just skilled, he was crazy; he was not just crazy, he was skilled. Max pulled himself into a desperate duck, rolled himself out and up into the clear.

"You leave my old man alone," the woman shrieked. She flew at Max, hands up like claws, and snatched at his face and hair.

"Get outa the way, Rain," Tyrone panted.

Max batted at her arms.

"Leave him alone!" She sounded like a fire siren. Her fingernails caught cheek skin just above Max's beard.

"Rain!"

"Get her off me. I might hurt her," Max managed.

"Male chauvinist *piiiig!*" She got a grip on his ear and twisted it vigorously.

Max slapped her hard. She fell down. He felt blood trickling down his neck. He gasped, trying to control the violent cramping in his stomach. Tyrone knelt by his wife; he slapped at her with the backs of his hands.

"Don't you ever got in my way like that again, you hear me? Bitch! Bitch!"

Max held onto the light pole and retched.

A gang of people came out of the bar and stood looking at them from across the street.

"Hey Max," someone yelled. Max couldn't see that far. He pressed his head against the cold light pole. Another wave of heaves threatened to overwhelm him. He had managed to get a handkerchief from his back pocket and press it against his ear.

"Not like you to beat up a woman," the voice said, coming closer.

"Get away from her," Tyrone screamed. He pulled Rain to her feet and they walked away together.

"Jesus Christ! What'd she do to you?" It was Dennis, one of Max's Brooklyn College students.

"I'm...okay," he said.

"Jesus. You oughta see a doctor."

"It's okay."

"Can I take you home? You look awful. You really oughta see a doctor."

"It's...don't worry." Max let go of the pole and took a few experimental steps. It wasn't fun. He could keep going though. Dennis walked beside him, peering seriously into Max's face.

"Jesus, Max, what happened? You want a cab or something? I could take you to St. Vincent's. Holy shit, your ear's bleeding like crazy."

"Be quiet Dennis."

But Dennis left him alone only and finally when Max had unlocked the tinned-over door to the stairs to his loft, stopped in the hall, and shut the street door (gently) in the young man's strained, eager-to-be useful pink freckled face.

The hall was lit by twenty-five watt light bulbs, one per landing. They were smoky yellow in the dusty air. As Max began the five-flight climb tears ran down his cheeks the way water runs from a low-pressure garden hose. If the tears were from pain or something close to rage, or plain fatigue, or sorrow for the whole damn mess of everything—Max was in no condition to tell.

Morning Sorrow

The morning light was cold slate gray. Max picked his head up fast, trying to figure out where be was. Too fast. He groaned involuntarily, managed to muffle the noise as throbs raced through his body, and realized he was on the daybed in the loft. His shirt was clammy with old sweat, his feet swollen inside his boots. He tested himself out, slowly: everything hurt but everything worked. He swung his feet out and sat up. A covered casserole sat on the kitchen counter and next to it a platter, stacked with rolls and covered with a napkin. There were also two new loaves of bread, neatly wrapped in waxed paper. The scent of baked bread hovered.

Women always cook when there's a death; curious. Max put his hand on one of the loaves—it was cool. It's not only to feed the living, he decided, but to reaffirm the realness of being alive. He walked quietly around the partition. Betsy was sleeping in a curled ball up on the loft bed; he could see the top of her head and hear her snoring softly. He stripped himself of his stinking clothes. His body felt a hundred years old; he wondered how many days it would take before his bones stopped aching as he took robe and towel and padded quietly to the hall where the shower was.

He took a long time under the water and then examined himself in the mirror for visible damage noting only dark grey circles under his eyes, a few scratch marks on his cheek. The ear that had bled so much had a tiny rip at the top. He dabbed at the spot with a bit of peroxide and combed his hair.

Betsy was still sleeping when he returned. He pinched one of her cigarettes and sat in the easy chair by the daybed with it. The early morning light from the windows was the same color as his cigarette smoke. He wanted to climb the loft bed ladder, wake her up, take her, soft and boneless as a kitten, groggy and protesting at first, responding as she woke to him...but his own body protested. Even his thoughts worked against desire; they rattled like fruits in a slot machine.

Charlene had a secret that needed keeping; it was in more danger of leaking out with Shirley dead. If Marcia's account was accurate, Charlene and Shirley had pulled off their fraud very neatly. The days of Charlene's fame and consequent dependency were over—unless, Max thought, someone had plans for something new from Charlene. Not impossible. Charlene or her associates might want the potential bomb Shirley represented to be defused permanently. That was improbable but not impossible. He continued with it.

Suppose it had dawned on Dick Conway that Shirley was using him? It seemed to Max she had been—as coldly as she had used Charlene. He'd made her a lot of money, but was she really going into marriage with him? Dick was a liar by inclination and by training but retaliation would be his style—not murder. He had been defeated by her death; he felt impotent because of it. Still, he and Tyrone had been rivals for control of her decisions. Max had put his body in between the two of them and gotten what interlopers get. He stubbed the cigarette out angrily.

Tyrone. It was illogical for him to kill his sister; she was his golden goose. Ah, but a fool killed the Golden Goose, he remembered. Tyrone might have started something that went out of control. From his experience last night, that was not impossible at all.

What else was going on in Shirley's life to bring it to such a conclusion? How much did any one person know about her? People can live intricately faceted lives, especially in cities. Close friends who know one interface may know nothing at all about the existence of the others. He thought of a painter he had known well for five years before discovering, through an unrelated friendship with a neighborhood TV repairman who was an amateur chess buff that the painter was supported, not by sales of his art but by an elderly woman, quite distinguished in chess circles. The painter slept with her every Sunday morning. They spent the rest of the day analyzing chess games together.

The only person Max was completely sure of was Robby Rosen, sitting in the Putnam County lock-up. Damn, he'd promised to call Georgia Phipps at eight o'clock last night—about the time that Tyrone Pendergast had been making mincemeat of his liver and lights. It was Saturday morning now, early; she'd be home, sleeping.

"Max? Are you okay Max?" Betsy's face was as rumpled as her hair. She squinched her eyes, trying to focus.

"Hi," Max said.

"God damn you!"

"Bets, don't point your finger that way. You look like a schoolmarm."

Her face went through a series of expressions like a driver shifting in a drag race. The top gear was a puzzled mixture of concern and disappointment. A bit sour, Max felt, looking at her mouth, but then he had certainly handed her the short end of it.

"You didn't come home, you didn't call. I called the bar, they said you'd left."

"I came home."

"Well, I waited here a while. Then I went upstairs to Cinda's. I even left you a note but you didn't call. When I came in you were passed out cold. Max, did you fall down or something? You scared me to death. I actually woke you up trying to clean your face, but I bet you don't you remember."

"I was pretty drunk."

"You were out of your head. And there was a lot of blood. For chrissake, will you tell me."

"I got drunk with Dick Conway. Don't be a baby, Betsy, I'm sorry I scared you. You ready to get up? I'll make breakfast."

No reply. Max's bare skin was cold suddenly. He pulled on his bathrobe tighter and went to the kitchen stove.

"Max, you can't believe how awful it is over there. I mean about Siddy. Shirley's parents are worse than even she ever said. Uptight, self-righteous! They've got about as much sympathy for kids as a stick of wood. They acted as if Ocean and Ellen and Milo were vermin – and Siddy? You could nearly hear the word 'nigger' when they looked at her."

Max lit the stove, pulled out the coffee bean grinder instead of reaching for the instant.

"Mitzi and Lynn—well, I suppose they got the drift that, you know, that there aren't any men in their lives." (Hard not to, Max thought, with their hallway and bathroom plastered full of Lesbian posters.) "I mean there's the obvious solution, but they wouldn't think of it, not ever. If they hadn't had to go do this and that with lawyers and police and all, I think they'd have taken Sidney with them yesterday afternoon. It's scary."

"Solution?" Max asked. Getting breakfast organized was more of a challenge than he'd bargained for.

"Mitzi and Lynn love Sidney. It's a household full of kids. They know her, she knows them. She could even go on going to her own school, keep her friends. Mitzi and Lynn just—they'd do anything to keep her. Mitzi would adopt her legally if the Pendergasts would let her. But all they see is the wrath of god, unnatural women, that sort of thing. It's, it's … what can be done?"

"Not much, honey. They are her grandparents."

"Max. We can't just sit by and let a child be tortured!"

"Aren't you being dramatic?"

"You don't mean that!"

"She's lost her mother. It's gonna be hard on the kid no matter what," Max pointed out.

"She doesn't have to live with people who're ashamed of her. I heard Mr. Pendergast actually used the word 'pickaninny.'"

"Give them a chance. They're probably in shock." The whirr of the coffee grinder kept him from hearing her answer.

". . .straight couple wanted to keep her?" Betsy had a guarded look. She was sitting cross-legged, leaning forward as she watched his face.

"No!" Max said. "I didn't hear what you said and my answer's no."

She went into the other room and began to dress.

"You're going to want kids someday, Max." Her voice was a bit muffled; she was leaning over fastening her shoes. Max turned and leaned on the sink. A drop of water oozed out of the faucet, grew globular at its base, held, shimmering and swelling, then broke free, smashing its perfect form to pieces on the white porcelain below. He shoved the handles back firmly. No. No. No.

They passed each other as he went to the closet-space underneath the loft bed. Betsy had chosen a dress, her interview-for-a teaching-job costume, a dark green fitted smock. She'd put on stockings. Max took slacks instead of jeans. He was having a hard time choosing a shirt.

"Max?" Her voice was wheedling, hurt.

"Betsy, no. No."

"I was only going to ask if you were hungry. I just want coffee."

If he said 'don't lie' he'd open the question up again. If he said nothing, it would sit there, ugly and swelling, like a boil, a sore that pained both of them. He chose cowardice and a dark blue shirt.

"Just coffee suits me fine," he said softly.

She backed off too: "You really don't think anything can be done?"

"I really think the Pendergasts deserve some time. Maybe some help. Instead of everybody jumping to conclusions."

"You'll feel differently when you see it. The situation."

"Okay."

They drank coffee for a time, discussed transportation of the food. Betsy packed everything tenderly in a shopping bag and agreed they needed a taxicab uptown. Max was locking the door when he remembered Georgia Phipps again.

A Small Backfire

It was not quite ten o'clock. Betsy was at the bottom of the stairs, waiting for him but Max had stopped in the loft to make a call. The phone was answered by a man, froggy-voiced with sleep. Max apologized.

"S'all right," the voice demurred. "Good you called. I think Georgia's got a bone to pick with you, matter of fact."

Max waited, trying to interpret the muffled noises on the other end.

"Max Birtwhistle?" She was crisp and high, nothing morning-mist about her. "You'd have helped me and your friend Rosen a good deal more if you'd been more frank with me yesterday."

Max didn't answer.

"Are you there? Are you there?"

"Yeah. I'm waiting to hear what's happened."

"I put my friend Donald in a very embarrassing position. He's furious. You should have told me Rosen is irrational."

"If he is, I'm sorry to hear it. Explain what's happened, will you?"

"I'm afraid you'll have to tell me. I haven't seen the man. I don't know him. Donald says frankly he can't tell if Rosen's putting on an act or not. The point is there's another lawyer already there. I asked a friend to do a favor and I've made him look as if he's poaching clients from someone else. Ignorantly, too, without solid understanding of what he was getting into. Rosen was rude, completely uncooperative, crazed! Nothing from him but one contradictory statement after another. He's got the authorities so freaked they've put him in an isolation cell on suicide watch. Donald says he'd do the same."

"Oh Christ," Max groaned.

"They may try to send him over to the state hospital for observation. Believe me, Birtwhistle, it's easier to bail out a felon with a record as long as your arm than it is to get a client out from under the state's headshrinkers. Do you know what's going on?"

"Has he been talking about a Heppmeyer or a guy called Schmidt?"

"Not that I've heard. Exactly what did you not tell me?"

Max held the phone a little away from his ear. Not that she was screaming exactly, her volume was moderate, but each word snapped.

"Not much—they're characters in his novel. He sometimes talks about the people he's invented. Where did this other lawyer come from? What happens now?"

There was a pause. Max could hear her breathing rapidly.

"Curious how I simply don't believe you."

"That's because you're very smart." Max grinned. He couldn't help it.

"Listen, Birtwhistle,"

"Please, it's Max. I'm calling you Georgia."

"Don't ever call me by any name if you're not willing to be frank. All the way, bottom line."

"What happens to Robby now?" Max persisted.

"He's up for trespassing on a crime scene this Monday morning, providing he keeps himself out of a padded cell. He'll get off with a fine—unless they have enough for something else by then. Let's say arson, felony murder, burglary. . . . He must be expecting something stronger than spitting on the street. He's working awful hard to cop insanity." In spite of herself, Georgia sounded a bit interested. "You think he's calculating too, don't you?"

"I don't know. I don't know what he's thinking."

"Next time, get your story straight before you try to get help for him." She said this bare of any inflection. It was a statement of ordinary fact.

"Georgia, thanks, I mean it. I'm sorry everything got so bolloxed up..." The phone clicked off before he'd even said "sorry." He finished his sentence anyway, looked into the humming receiver for a moment longer, then delicately placed it back on its hook.

Betsy had come back up the steps and had been listening.

"I've got to go back up to Putnam County, Bets."

"Max!"

"I can't let it alone. Robby's getting himself in a hell of a mess."

"You mean now?" Her eyes glittered like steel ball bearings, and slender cords stood out on her neck.

"No." He was thinking rapidly. 'Everyone' is coming up to Lynn's house Betsy had told him: Would that be thirty people? fifty? How much did anybody else know?

"Robby's scared," he continued, "he may have fiction mixed up with reality but he's really scared. As far as I can tell, over nothing. I've gotta try and help him."

"Today?" she demanded. "Today!"

"I'll fix it. I'll come with you."

"Don't patronize me," she exploded. "If you're concerned about Robby, well I'm concerned about Sidney. And she's a child. Besides, Shirley was a friend of mine. Yours too, I thought. This is for her, you know."

"I'm sorry. I seem to be saying everything wrong."

"The whole thing sounds wrong. I heard you say that Robby talks about his characters! Robby never, absolutely never, discusses what he's working on. We had a long talk about it once. He says everything has to go onto a page; talking about it would wreck his concentration."

"I lied," Max rubbed his head. "Robby is convinced some Nazis are after him. The less said about it the better."

Betsy's mouth opened. She put her hand to it. "Is it true?"

"Doesn't appear to be. That's the problem. One of the problems. I met brother Tyrone last night. He's a problem for sure."

"You met him?"

"On the street. Seems he's been trying to make Shirley give him money. I'd like to talk to the senior Pendergasts too. Are they supposed to be there?"

"Well they don't think much of the memorial but they're supposed to be coming to pick up Sidney. I want to talk to them too. *If* I can. See if I can talk them into at least letting Siddy stay here a little longer. I hope you're right about them but I just don't think so."

"So we go," said Max. He picked up the shopping bag and the two of them made their way out onto the street.

The elevator smelled of dog pee and stale cigarette smoke. The building it was in had once been a decorously appointed upper-middleclass high rise. When it was new, fifty years ago, it had had a doorman, an elevator operator, and two or three hall porters, all in uniforms and gloves, all paid to smile at the ladies and gentlemen who left their children with a live-in maid and took taxi cabs to dinner parties and the theatre.

Now, the door opened with a buzzer squawk-box system; the cavernous lobby was stripped of everything but its decorative tile, a long mirror bolted to the walls, and a foolish-looking ornamental fireplace. The walls were liberally looped with spray can graffiti. Over and under it were taped posters claiming cures for present ills: Rent strike now! March against war and racism, Try meditation, Christian fellowship group, Learn to play bamboo flute. Inside the elevator yet another sign begged "Adorable kittens, free! Ring apartment 12-C" to which someone had added, "Want pussy? Call Francine" with a phone number, but someone else had scratched the number out. Lynn and Mitzi's place was on the 16th floor, just below the penthouses. The elevator clanked as it rose.

Mitzi checked them through the spy hole first, then rattled at the chain and dead bolt. She rubbed her cheek against Betsy's wordlessly, then took the shopping bag from Max, smiling but cautious. Max reciprocated.

"I'm making a ham," she told Betsy, "and a big fruit salad. I hope there'll be enough."

They followed her down the long hall, past bedrooms arranged like the cars on a little train, and turned into the fat L-shaped kitchen. Mitzi had a dancer's body, tight and well disciplined. Her long blonde hair hung in a fat braid down her small muscular back. But she hadn't danced since just before Ellen was born, six years ago. She'd carried a lot on that back since then, Max thought. To repay Ellen's dad for marrying her, she'd dropped out of dancing, juggling secretarial job and baby care while her husband studied architecture. A second pregnancy had made her ill. She miscarried and recovered to take on still more guilt—crippling doctor bills and smothered grief for the loss of a second child her husband had not really wanted. He was the one who had the breakdown—he failed his exams, and began to drink. She had squared her angular shoulders once again, gotten a second job, and taken herself and him to family therapy and alcohol clinics. Her efficient anger must have been terrifying.

According to Betsy, the husband has a new wife now, an infant boy, and a comfortable administrator's job at a community college on Long Island. He's bitter about the child support he has to pay, insisting, angrily and unreasonably, that Ellen, now age six, is not his child.

"She never touched another man," Betsy said heatedly. "He just can't deal with the fact she really loves women."

"There's nothing harder," Max had answered dryly. "You women don't want to recognize how scared us men are."

"Wan a teazle?" A tiny girl child strode into the kitchen. Max was standing quietly by the door, looking helpful but actually trying to keep out of the way. Betsy and Mitzi were slicing bread, sorting crackers, chopping fruits, stacking dishes and arranging platters. They exchanged monosyllables as they worked around the large eating table.

"Absolutely," Max answered, squatting by the doorjamb.

"Can't eat it." The warning was grave, intent. The child's eyes protruded under her beetling black eyebrows. She looked like a feminine miniature of Lorenzo d'Medici, the bent nose, the wide mouth, the rampant bandit-like intelligence shining through her ugly face. Her name was Milo; she was Lynn's daughter.

"He think you can eat it," she said scornfully. She pointed up the hall to the big living room. Max could hear two children's voices breaking into screams of argument.

"They've been fighting all morning," Mitzi said wearily.

Milo opened her grubby fist for Max to see. It held a dead waterbug, on the back of which she had attached a tiny lump of pink playdough.

"Ick," Betsy grunted, looking down.

"Oh, you know Milo," Mitzi answered.

Max transferred the trophy to his flattened palm with two careful fingers. There was a crash and a piercing scream from the front of the apartment.

"Mother, Motherrrr!"

A stocky little boy on a plastic tricycle careened through the living room's open French doors and pedaled furiously down the long hall. The ancient parquet squeaked from the stress.

"Rescue, rescue!" he shouted hoarsely.

Ellen raged into the kitchen, bumping Milo against the table leg and causing Max to close his hand protectively around Milo's creation. Ellen had scratch marks on her hand; she was holding a crumpled doll, "He ran over 'ivtabel. Make him *stop*. Shit head!" She thrust the doll at her mother and raced down the hall after the little boy. She was sitting on his head by the time Mitzi reached them. Ocean was kicking violently, his stubby brown boots barely missing her knees, and both of them were bellowing.

"Fucker," Ellen hollered.

"Poop head, poop head," Ocean chanted, muffled by her body.

Mitzi separated the two of them from each other and the upturned tricycle, holding them, with a hand on each chest, on opposite sides of the hallway. They waited for her response, their faces painfully flushed with frustration and fear.

"He..." Ellen began.

"Kids—" Mitzi dropped her hands and began to cry, "Kids, I'm sorry."

"She pushed my *head*" Ocean croaked pleadingly, worry in his round blue eyes.

"He scratched me, Mitzi." Ellen held her hand out. She stroked her mother's arm, and tears began rolling down her face as well.

"Come in the bedroom with me," Mitzi gulped, taking their hands.

"I can handle things in here," Betsy called. "The ham's doing fine."

Mitzi vanished into the first bedroom with Ellen,

pulling Ocean behind her. He'd gone limp, like a civil rights protestor, allowing himself to be dragged on his rump. He was now crying too.

"Shirley died" Milo said.

"Yes," Max answered. He opened his hand. "I'm afraid I mashed it." He returned the bug. "Let's go in the living room and see if you can fix it."

Three wide front windows, with safety bars, let in sky, the tops of buildings, a wedge of Hudson River, and brown New Jersey beyond, serrated with condominiums. The windows held woven wall hangings carefully installed above the reach of children's fingers. The boundary was clear; on the wall smudge marks and scrubbed out crayon scribbles reached only so high. Above to the high white ceiling, the room was pristine, airy and unblemished. Below lay the region of child pollution, like the low cloud that lies over a city. Shelving made with planks and bricks obviously intended to contain children's possessions stretched along the whole left side of the room. Multi-colored stuff disgorged from them. Pillows and toys, socks and school books, abandoned dishes of cereal and half-eaten fruits. Milo stepped delicately over spilled tinker toys and placed her creature on top of the shelf. She examined it, rekneading the speck of play dough.

Max took a plastic airplane out of the goldfish bowl and set it to dry in the sun.

"Hello Lynn. Hi Siddy," he said. Through the archway to another, smaller room he could see Lynn sitting in a rocking chair. Sidney was in her lap. They faced a small television set, blinking a cartoon show, but Lynn was reading to the child from a large green book. He went toward them.

Sidney's perfect oval face was marred by circles underneath her eyes. Her mocha complexion had a greenish cast. Her huge dark eyes absorbed all light; they did not shine. Lynn jumped a little at the greeting and looked up hesitantly. Lynn was painfully shy.

"We're reading *The Wizard of Oz*," she said. "Sidney's like Dorothy, I think. Brave and kind, like she is." She stroked the girl's crinkly hair. Sidney's expression didn't change but she snuggled, just perceptibly, against Lynn's luxuriant breasts.

#

Four women arrived together with bowls of food, tears, kisses, hugs. Together with Shirley, the eight of them had met formally as a consciousness raising group. After a time, the formal group had given way to a sort of network, maintained mostly by long telephone calls. Betsy was the only member who had remained attached to a straight male mate. The others, either before or early in their group friendship, had declared themselves gay. Max wondered again, when Betsy again failed to introduce him, if she apologized to them for that. He knew the names of only two of them: Victoria and Jensie. They were all measured or deliberately casual with him.

Mitzi wanted chairs arranged in rows in the living room. Betsy, with a sort of girl-scout expression on her face, was a baffled but loyal lieutenant. There was a buzz of cross talk as they struggled with private recollections for models to follow or discard for a memorial and simultaneously for best strategies for clearing the room for this function. Max offered to help move Mitzi's heavy wooden loom across to the dining room to make more space. Jensie glared at him. She and the skinny woman in blue pants hoisted it without him.

"I've invited Horace Daniels to speak," Mitzi announced abruptly. "He's nonsectarian," she assured her friends. "Choose some records, Betsy," she commanded as she ran toward the splashing thuds coming from the bathroom. Ocean and Milo were supposed to be bathing.

"Mitzi, how could you?" One of the women shouted after her. Her heavy handmade earrings swung with emotion. Under her plump arms dark sweat stains had begun to streak her embroidered green blouse. "He didn't even know Shirley. That's nuts. Mitzi, *you* ought to speak."

"I think it's okay," Betsy offered.

Max knelt, stuffing game pieces inefficiently into what was probably the wrong box, wishing desperately for a belt of bourbon.

"Who is this bimbo anyway?" Jensie demanded. She was intense and thin with a sunken face and a huge mop of scraggly unkempt hair.

Max looked up. She hadn't meant him.

"He's head of the Church of Human Fellowship," Betsy explained. "It's over on West End Avenue. He's okay, really. Mitzi knows him."

"Someone from a church, what a crock. Shirley hated church."

Lynn sat heavily on the couch. "Oh please don't argue,"

she begged, but so softly that only Max, kneeling by the shelves could hear her. Max looked up at her and smiled. She blushed and turned her face away with a nervous jerk. Lynn looked like Mother Earth: powerful, dominating, broad-shouldered. Her blue-black hair coiled on her head like a crown and her lush body radiating energy. Lynn dwelled inside this edifice, Max thought, like a mouse inside a Sherman tank.

The front door buzzer rang. The women panicked; they were not "ready."

To hell with this, Max decided. He went into the kitchen and methodically rummaged cabinets. In the third from the wall he found a sherry bottle, poured a belt into a paper cup, and nearly choked. It was cooking sherry, liberally salted. He gargled tap water at the sink. There was a small giggle. Milo was sitting on the floor watching him. She was naked and dripping wet. She had a small bunch of grapes balanced on her knees.

"Aren't you cold?" he asked.

"No." She spit a grape seed into the puddle that had collected around her.

"But your toes are blue."

She inspected them. "That's dirt, you know."

Max went back to his search.

"Oh, there you are." Betsy poked her head in the door. She had a towel in her hand. "Come on, Milo. The Webbers have brought their little boy."

"I don't like to," Milo said.

The buzzer bell went off again.

"Max, don't lurk in the kitchen," Betsy said brightly. She scooped the child into the towel.

"But I don't like to," Milo repeated patiently as Betsy toted her down the hall. She shook her head resignedly over Betsy's shoulders. Max shrugged at her. They turned off into Milo's room as Max continued down the hall to answer the front door.

A white woman in a blue suit in her early fifties, with bronzed hair and pale pink lipstick, and a man in a navy suit, very black-skinned and very scented with expensive men's cologne, were waiting in the hall. They were colleagues of Shirley's from Wilson-Hill, they said. They were terribly grieved, they said in lowered voices, and very glad they had been asked to come. The woman was holding a boxed bottle of Cutty Sark. Max could have kissed her.

But his plan to make off with it was foiled. The elevator disgorged a half a dozen other people and by the time Max had ushered the newcomers in, the two Wilson-Hill people were sitting together on one of the couches and their bottle was nowhere in sight.

More people came but everyone stuck together in little knots, talking quietly to the people they'd come with. A lugubrious folk song trio emanated from the record player. Food was spread out on a long table in the dining room but no one was eating; the giant coffee urn Victoria had lugged in sputtered erratically, its "not-ready" light glowing. Max sat on a folding chair and closed his eyes. Could that record have been Shirley's? It was a total relic.

"Max!" Mike Cowber sat beside him. He patted Max fondly on the back. "What do you think," he asked, quietly opening his jacket just enough to display six neat joints of marijuana in his inside breast pocket.

"I don't think so," Max said. "You never know."

The buzzer was ringing again.

"I wanna go say hi to Betsy," Mike said, sliding off.

And I better go to work, Max thought. It wasn't so different from gallery parties. He went the rounds, introducing himself, trying to pick up pieces of information. Marcia Jennings jumped up and clung to his arm. She was developing a crush. She was awfully worried about Robby, she told him, dewy-eyed. Max promised to call her at the office on Monday, ducking the offer of her home phone number.

The faces fell into place: business friends from several publishing companies, an agent, a secretary, a short-story writer. The imposing man with heavy horn rims and thick greying eyebrows turned out to be Shirley's psychiatrist but, he assured Max in a rumbling professional tone, he had no light to shed on her personal life. He would certainly cooperate with the authorities (and not with you, he meant) if he knew anything at all that might help their investigations. As Max was listening to a gushy young man reminisce about literary people he was much too young to have known personally, he felt a gentle pressure on his arm. A small balding man stood at his elbow. Sad round baby's eyes looked gravely out of his middle-aged face. He wore a dark grey suit with a neatly folded paisley handkerchief in its pocket. His fingers were deeply stained from nicotine.

"Can we talk a second"" he asked apologetically.

He and Max walked together to one of the big front windows. He lit a cigarette and looked out across the rooftops. He was Abraham Glazer he said. He lived in the apartment just below Shirley's. He loved her, he said simply. But they were only friends. He loved her distance, her precision, the measured discipline of her life. He shrugged and smiled, bobbing his oval head. He knew a lot about her, more than many of her friends. The two of them talked. He was a film editor and often worked at an editing table in his apartment. Late at night they used to order Chinese food together and hash out professional problems, fascinated by the similarities and differences in their crafts. He recognized instantly that Max was on the prowl for information – and he apparently knew quite a bit about Max and Betsy. Anything he could do to help find the people responsible. . . . His soft voice was edged with anger.

Max asked about her ex-husband first. Shirley had tried to find him about a year ago, Glazer reported. Not for money but because of Sidney. She hadn't been able to find a trace. The man had dropped from sight, cut his connections absolutely, quite probably changed his name. He thought Max ought to know, though, Shirley had a boyfriend in Putnam County.

"Boy friend?" Max asked.

"Bed friend, you know," He coughed a little as a flood of smoke poured from his nose and blew up across his face.

"Did Dick Conway know about him?"

"That's the point. Shirley didn't think so. He wasn't supposed to. The thing is, I can't remember his name. In fact, I'm not sure Shirley ever told me and I certainly would never have asked. A young guy though, I'm sure of that."

"Was Shirley really planning to marry Dick?"

Glazer laughed unpleasantly.

Max asked about Tyrone.

"Oh no," he whispered. He looked hurt. "She wasn't worried by him. I'd have known. She. . . . Conway is a creep," he said suddenly in a more certain tone. "A damn nuisance. She was trying to get rid of him, believe me. An emotional leech, I'd call him. And a liar. I don't think you should believe anything he says."

"Oh Christ," Max said tersely, turning his head. Dirty Jack was in the doorway. Max edged away from the window, hoping he wouldn't be recognized but the man ploughed across the room and grabbed his arm.

"Man," Jack breathed, stretching his thin mouth over his wine-stained teeth. "Some scene, huh?"

"Yeah, it's a real drag, Jack."

"How ya been, huh? Where you keep yourself?"

"Here and there," Max answered, "You know how it is."

Glazer flashed Max a sympathetic look and dissolved into the crowd. Max walked deliberately to the middle of the room but Jack's grip on his arm stayed firm.

"Not like the old days, huh ... down on Third Street... Shirl and David. Hey, man, I saw Ellie other week. Blow, you know. You really oughtta ... "

"It's hard for me," Max interrupted.

Jack's gaze was feverish, his lank hair was pushed back between two balding vee's that had grown wider since Max saw him last. A girl who was hanging a step or two behind him was very young. She'd be, knowing Jack, not more than seventeen but she looked as exhausted as her companion. Her eyes glittered and she smiled violently. Her hair was an odd purple color.

"I got some dynamite stuff to read," Jack said, gesturing at his soiled shoulder bag. "Cookin, you known, things are cook-ken. Lissen. . ."

How does he do it, Max wondered, looking at Jack's ravaged face. Almost eighteen years ago he looked so spent and ill no one thought he'd live another year. His hair thins, his paunch gets puffier - and he'll come to *my* funeral with a drug-sick high school girl and a batch of stoned-out poems to read. Jack waved a spiral notebook, gabbling incomprehensibly. His girl smiled on. Marcia, standing nearby, gaped, horrified.

With a flourish of noisy emotion, Charlene Burke swept into the room, flanked by three large black men. Two of them were decked out in Harlem's best pimp style: platform shoes, bold patterned jackets across their accentuated shoulders, jewels on fingers, wide-brimmed felt hats trimmed with silks and feathers. The third was in African dress – a bright dashiki and coarse sandals. His tense dark face was completely encircled by fuzzy afro and fuzzy beard. The white people in the room backed away, giving them center stage. They filled it willingly.

"You," Charlene boomed. She came toward Max with her long arms outstretched. "Low-down skunk, ain't that so." She gave him a muscular, completely unexpected hug. She was almost as tall as he was; in her arms Max felt small. He struggled to right himself.

"Fiah inspector," Charlene drawled. "You give *them* a turn or two." Her men surrounded them. Max shook hands and nodded politely at each. Marcia had disappeared.

"But I am inspecting," he said deliberately.

Charlene's face was smooth, unflinching. "Thass your story," she said.

"I don't like murder," Max answered.

She shook her head at him. "Whoooee," she said to her men, "Get him." The man in the dashiki looked insulted; the two others snickered.

"I need some help," Max said.

"I needa see that poor child," Charlene cut him off. The four moved together. Max intervened.

"Not all of you, unless Sidney knows you."

"He's right," Charlene told the men and followed Max alone to the door of Ellen's room. There was talking inside and Max pushed the door gently, seeing first Lynn's face, who put a warning finger to her lips, and then Sidney and Ellen sitting beside a bearded young man who was squatting by the bed. Sidney's teacher, Lynn whispered. Max gestured to Charlene to take a look, then he closed the door.

"Wanna wait a bit. The kid's pretty shaky," he said. The hall was empty. "Charlene," Max began, "what's Rashid's part in this, do you know?" Charlene's lip curled a little. "He ...," she looked up. Mitzi surged toward them.

"You're Charlene Burke, aren't you," Mitzi blurted intently.

Charlene nodded.

"I'm Mitzi Greenspan, Shirley's friend. I've got to talk to you. We have a big problem with Sidney. You know about this, Max. We've got to *do* something. Shirley's parents are coming soon to take her away. We can't let them. They..." she faltered, a blush spreading across her cheeks. "You know, they don't want...it's..."

"I hear what you're saying," Charlene answered unexpectedly.

"She's got a father," Max interjected.

"Well he don't want her cause she's white," Charlene snapped. "You getting' just what you asked for, ain't you?"

"I never asked for anything," Mitzi exploded. "That's no answer."

"Naw, none of you did nothing. That's all we hear. It ain't *my* fault, it ain't *my* fault..."

"You know that for a fact?" Max interrupted. "About Rashid?"

Charlene's black eyes were burning. "I don't know nothing. He disappeared. No one seen him in a year, probably ain't even in this country."

"Venice?" Max reminded her.

"Yeah, where's that, in Italy? They got a bad check rap on him. You get what I'm saying? He is *gone*." Anger rolled in her voice, echoing in the long hallway.

Several people had now collected in the doorway to the living room. The bearded man in the dashiki pushed past them. Betsy followed. Mitzi looked up into Charlene's enraged face and burst into tears. She made a dash for the bathroom; when she opened the door, Max got a glimpse of Mike Cowber sitting on the tub rim, smoking peacefully. Max went in the other direction.

"It's okay, Bets," he said, passing her, touching her arm, "I'm gonna get some coffee."

The buzzer bell was ringing again. Of course it was Dick. He was crocked, again or still, and he clutched a three-foot tall stuffed teddy bear, wrapped elaborately in orange cellophane, against his rumpled cashmere jacket.

"Siddy knows," he shouted shrilly, "She's the only one who knows the way I feel."

Betsy, bless her, had the presence of mind to shove him into the kitchen, give him a cup of coffee, and stay there with him. Through the rumble of talk in the living room, Max could hear his voice, edged with pleading, Siddy this, Siddy that—and Betsy's voice, only once, sharply telling him to stop being difficult.

When the Reverend Horace Daniels of the Church of Human Fellowship turned up at last, almost forty minutes late, Mitzi and Mike Cowber, and Lynn with Ellen, Ocean, Milo and Sidney, and Max, too, reluctantly, all assembled themselves politely with the others and listened to him speak. He was perhaps twenty-eight, with picturesque black ringlets around his pale brown face. He waved his hands eloquently and spoke in rolling tones about the cycle of life and how love could break down the barriers of sex and race, and even, through its strength, "communicate through the gates of death" into the new place Shirley now inhabited. His chest muscles were beautifully developed, Max noted. The white turtleneck he wore stretched across them like a second skin and his heavy gold ankh rose and fell evenly. He breathed from the diaphragm like a singer, or a boxer, or an actor trained in Shakespeare.

The doorbell was ringing again and Mitzi scurried down the hall to answer as Daniels continued speaking about the human family drawing together in times of sorrow. But Mitzi didn't come back. Max slipped off his chair and went into the hall.

"If you prefer not to pay your respects to the people who loved your daughter, you can wait in here," she was saying rather shrilly, holding the door to Ellen's room open. Her face was scarlet, all the way down her neck.

The man she addressed turned a felt hat in nervously fidgeting fingers. His grey crew cut stood straight up, his seamed face was drawn into itself. He sucked his lower lip. In front of him stood a short woman with the high round forehead and short pointed nose she had passed on to both her children. She clutched a black pocketbook to her corsetted middle. She was the same height as Mitzi and she glared into her face, cold as ice.

"Just give us the child's things. We told you we were coming." She marched into Ellen's room. Tyrone and Rain followed the older couple. They were washed and combed. Rain was wearing a dress. She was also wearing a painful shiner on her right eye. The purple swelling ran well below her cheekbone and her other eye had shadowed slightly in sympathy. The bastard must have pasted her as hard as he can Max thought.

"Mary Frances," the man said tentatively.

"No," she answered stonily.

He tried again anyway: "She says they've got a *minister* in there…"

Tyrone gave Max a dead blank stare. Rain's one good eye looked terrified when she recognized him and she turned her head down to make her loose hair fall over her face for protection.

"You must be Shirley's parents," Max said, ignoring the younger pair. He told them his name and extended his hand. Mrs. Pendergast shook it gingerly with two cold fingers. Her husband gasped it with a hard good-guy grip.

"Sidney's in the big room with my wife and Shirley's

friends. We thought it might be good for her to be there for a small service..." He trailed off deliberately hoping the words 'wife' and 'service' would lessen the tension a degree or two.

"Can I get you anything? Some coffee?"

Mr. Pendergast looked grateful. He was about to answer when he caught his wife's pursed lips and swift shake of the head. He exhaled wordlessly and closed his mouth. She was surveying Ellen's room: a nineteenth-century missionary watching a defloration rite might have had an expression like hers. Max tried to look at it with her eyes. Instead of the pastel walls, ruffled curtains and bedspread she would find essential there was a room of anarchistic colors, tossed possessions, homemade artifacts. An open suitcase on the bottom bunk bed held some of Sidney's things. Max tried to think of something to say. He settled on a solicitous, "Please sit down Mrs. Pendergast."

Mitzi turned and left. From the big room the soothing tones of Reverend Daniels continued. Max plucked a leotard and a naked Raggedy Ann from a small easy chair. The doll had a clenched-fist "Women's Rights Now" button pinned to the heart on its chest and pubic hair had been drawn on the crotch in dark blue ink.

"Sit, Mary Frances, you look close to dropping," Mr. Pendergast urged uncertainly.

She'd die standing up, her face said. And no one was going to stop her.

"For god's sake, Dick!" someone shrieked. It was Betsy in the kitchen.

"Let go of the phone woman, this is serious," Dick bellowed.

Betsy squealed shrilly and chairs scraped in the living room. The Reverend Daniels' melodic flow of words halted.

"What's going on?" Mr. Pendergast asked.

Max ran into the kitchen and locked Dick's arm tightly behind him. He put his left leg in front of Dick's right one ready to kick it out from under him. Betsy was backed against the kitchen wall phone. She had a red mark on one arm, her lips were grey, and she was shaking.

"Did he hit you?" Max pulled Dick's arm higher until he stopped squirming.

"Of course not, man," Dick gasped. "Call the police. The police, for chrissake. He's here!" His face was purpling.

"No," Betsy managed. "Get him out of here," she begged Max.

"You walking or do I break your back?" Max hissed. The door of the kitchen was jammed with gaping faces. The two of them struggled briefly until Dick went limp.

"I'm walking," he shrieked, "You stupid son of a bitch."

Max let go. He felt sick to his stomach and his vision blurred a moment.

"To the nearest phones," Dick shouted straightening up. "I think you've lost your mind."

Max gripped his elbow and steered him down the hall.

"Get her some whiskey and make her sit down," he barked to no one in particular, gesturing at Mrs. Pendergast who stood stricken in Ellen's doorway. Tyrone and Rain remained in place behind her. Max pushed Dick down the hall and out of the front door.

"Max!" Dick said.

"No!" Max slammed the door; the chain clattered noisily in the shocked silence.

"Please," Mitzi said.

"Please," whispered Lynn. She threaded her way through the crowd spilling into the hallway from the living room. She was carrying Sidney. The child's long legs bumped limply against Lynn's knees. She was sobbing and the shoulder of Lynn's blouse was soaked with tears. They went into the bathroom.

Everyone had cried. The guests, pale and shaken, had fled, the Reverend Daniels barely saying goodbye. Sidney pleaded, "but I want to stay with Lynn," and even Mrs. Pendergast had tears like icicles standing on her cheeks.

Max closed suitcases, called taxis, and then dried dishes while Betsy tried to comfort Lynn and Mitzi who sobbed into the soapsuds as they struggled to clean up. He could barely remember coming home, holding Betsy against him on the subway. The pieces scattered in his head, broken and disordered.

It had rained all night. Now it was pouring through the grey Sunday morning light and a foul smelling mist blew up between the drops as if instead of cleaning the air, the rain brought out its filth. Max held Betsy's hand in the almost empty bus watching the sodden streets lurch by. The hopelessness of their morning errand was a rock in his chest—but Betsy said she needed to try, and she needed him with her, and that was something he could do.

"Shit, my shoes must need new soles," Max said in the hotel elevator. Cold water was squishing up through his socks. Their rain slickers dripped steady streams of water onto the plush rug. He pointed down. "Wonder what do they do here when a dog takes a piss?" he grinned.

Betsy smiled thinly and he squeezed her hand. Mr. Pendergast opened the door.

"Can we come in a moment," Max asked swiftly

before the man could sort out the scattered emotions that played on his face.

"We just didn't want you to leave New York that way," Betsy said firmly. She smiled graciously, "We didn't think it was right."

"Who is it, Earl?"

He opened the door wide and gestured wordlessly toward the two of them. Sidney was sitting listlessly on an overstuffed easy chair. Her feet were in white socks and party shoes, the rest of her was wrapped in an overlarge blue bathrobe. Mrs. Pendergast stood behind her, a hairbrush and a glass of water in her hands. She'd been trying to make a part in Siddy's egg shaped Afro.

"It just won't stay *down*," she flustered crossly, almost as if Max and Betsy would disappear if she could avoid acknowledging them.

"May we come in?" Betsy persisted.

She set the hairbrush and water glass on an end table. "Our plane leaves at 3:15," she said finally.

"We won't stay long."

"Did you call the airport, Earl? I hope they're flying in this weather." Tension streaked her voice as she gave the grey world outside the hotel window a worried look.

Mr. Pendergast shut the room door. "I'm glad you came," he said huskily. He took their raincoats clumsily and went into the bathroom to hang them across the top of the sliding glass shower door.

Betsy went to the chair, stooped, and kissed Sidney gently on the cheek. "It's not supposed to stay down," Betsy explained. "It's the way it's cut."

"But it looks so wild," said Mrs. Pendergast.

"Well, if Siddy would like to, you could let it grow. Then you could braid it. Would you like braids, Siddy?" she asked. Sidney looked up at Betsy, impenetrable.

Mrs. Pendergast looked a little sick. "Wouldn't they stick up?" she whispered.

"Not unless you want them to," Betsy answered a shade tartly. "It's very obedient hair." She ran her fingers across the girl's soft fuzz. "It has a tendency to be dry though. Did you bring your hair lotion?" she asked the child. Sidney made no response.

Betsy drew in a breath. "Mrs. Pendergast, your granddaughter is who she is. She knows it. There's no point to thinking about her the way you do."

"I never. I never! No such thing." The woman's nose turned a little pink.

Sidney put her hands up to her head tentatively and then fluffed her hair vigorously until the attempted part disappeared. She sat very still when she'd finished, waiting.

Mrs. Pendergast looked down at her and sniffed. "You can get dressed now Sidney," she ordered. "I've put your things on my bed." The child slipped from the chair and disappeared into the other room. When the connecting door closed, Betsy began, "I know we all got off on the wrong foot with each other and I'm sorry. It's such a terrible thing. I...what I mean is, you see, we *all* feel it would be best for Sidney, it would help her adjust to all of this, if she at least finished school here this year. Where she knows everybody. Instead of trying to cope with so many changes all at once. You know what I mean? New home, new school." She took a breath. "Would you reconsider? Let Sidney stay with Mitzi and Lynn. Maybe come back for a longer visit later on this spring. Get to know her better before you take her to Ohio in the summer?"

Betsy stopped.

Max had never seen anyone literally wring their hands but Mrs. Pendergast did it now, twisting them painfully as if her problems could be squeezed away like dirty water.

"I can't leave my granddaughter in the care of perverts," she said at last. The twisting and pulling hands were unconnected to the soft flat tone of her voice.

"Please," Betsy said gently. She was controlling herself handsomely. "Lynn and Mitzi are both mothers. Wonderful mothers."

"It's disgusting," Mrs. Pendergast whispered. "What's wrong with this world anyway?" Her face was hard; she sat down in the easy chair. The hands in her lap kept working.

"We're punished. We're sorely tried," Mr. Pendergast announced. He sucked his lip. "I just can't see..."

"You can, Earl, you can. You teach your children right," she looked at Max, "teach them with a proper fear of God, bring them to Jesus, just as you should, but what can they hold on to? Everything is upside down. Praying in school is a crime but robbing and rioting is good. The Watergate wickedness has gone everywhere, everyone so angry, tearing things down, decent people are scared to go outside their doors!" She glared at Max as if she could command an explanation from him.

"Maybe it would help if you didn't judge so harshly!"

Betsy inserted. "If you tried to see that Lynn and Mitzi are human beings, *loving* human beings. They'd do anything for Sidney."

Mrs. Pendergast shot up from her seat. "*I* still know right from wrong," she shouted.

"Now, Mary Frances, please," her husband managed. His eyes flickered from Max to Betsy. "This is too much for her. Our daughter gone, our son, our son lost..." His eyes went back to Max. They were pleading.

"Where's your son now?" Max asked

"He won't listen to us, he hasn't heard our words for years."

"Is he still here, in New York?"

"I went on my knees last night. We did such a terrible thing. The man shook his head woodenly.

"What was that, Mr. Pendergast?"

"We shielded our son from the law. We lied before God and he's punished us."

Mrs. Pendergast covered her face with her hands.

"Tyrone killed a man. Now someone's killed our little girl." Mr. Pendergast's head hung and he mumbled this into his shirt.

"We never knew for sure," Mrs. Pendergast said brokenly from behind her hands.

"We knew, Mary Frances. We followed the papers for three days until they said the man had died. Then we said nothing. We never asked. We knew."

"Who was he?" Max asked.

"He worked in a filling station. Our son, our son hit him; he said so to me just last night."

"Did he hit Shirley too?" Max said this as softly as he

could. Mrs. Pendergast made a strangling noise behind her hands.

"Is that what you think?" Mr. Pendergast whispered. His face was a terrified yellow. His grief had not prepared him for this idea. Betsy put her arm across Mrs. Pendergast's shoulders and pushed her back into the chair. Her stocky little form went down as if it were tissue paper.

"It's possible," Max said. "Apparently he wanted Shirley to give him money and she'd told him no."

"The police seem to think this writer fellow did it. They've got him in the jail already." Mr. Pendergast was pleading almost childishly but not to Max. His eyes focused on an empty space in the middle of the room.

"Yes. I know. They're wrong about him."

"Tyrone never would hit Shirley!"

"He hit his wife," Max said. "Do you know where he is right now?"

"Gone home," the man mumbled. He pulled a brown address book from his jacket and gave it to Max. The leather cover was stamped "Compliments of Pendergast's Hardware."

"You're in the hardware business?" Max said as he copied the address.

"Thirty-five years. We started in the Great Depression, Mary Frances and me. We sold kettles and frying pans from door to door. Kept house in our truck first year or so. Opened up the store in 1943. Shirley was a tiny thing. You should have seen her when her mother curled her hair. She looked just like Shirley Temple. Everybody said so." His voice was drained. He spoke as if he'd memorized a text.

"Is there anyone back home to help you two?"

"We haven't told anyone about…" he stopped a moment, "about anything yet," he finished. "Find out it isn't so," he said suddenly. "Not Tyrone. Please. Call me." He thrust a business card into Max's hand.

"Call some friends before you leave New York. You can't do this by yourself."

The connecting door was open a few inches and Sidney was standing by the crack. Max wondered how long she'd been there.

Betsy poured water from a pitcher on the end table and handed the glass to Mrs. Pendergast.

Max went into the bathroom to get their raincoats.

"Mitzi thinks we could make a case." Betsy perched on a stool, chin in hands, her sharp elbows digging into her knees.

"Who's 'we'"?

She blushed.

"Well?" Max prodded. He was stuffing a sweater and thick hiking socks into his canvas overnight bag. The loft was dark even by the kitchen windows and outside the rain still fell, sluggish and thin, as though it took effort to drop through the late afternoon gloom.

"Shirley didn't want this to happen. Starkazi told Mitzi so. She just never got around to naming someone else as Siddy's guardian."

Max searched a drawer for his watch cap and gloves.

"Did you know she thought of asking us? Did you?"

Max slammed the drawer. He squelched the angry roar he wanted to release: Did any of you think of asking me?

"Max, why are you taking *all* that stuff?"

"It's March, Bets. They can get blizzards up there in March."

Betsy looked disbelieving. "You're taking enough for a month," she said grimly.

"I'm gonna get Robby out. I don't know how long it'll take. Somebody's got to get to the bottom of this."

"Well, Mitzi thinks we could make a case," Betsy repeated with narrowed eyes—"she, Mitzi."

"Is she talking about a custody fight? You've got to be

kidding. They're the child's natural grandparents."

"Well, Mitzi thinks we could make a case," she repeated.

"Yeah, in favor of a person never named by the mother as trustee for her estate. You can ask Starkazi yourself."

"They're not great characters, y'know. They're the parents of a murderer!"

"You don't lose your rights for uncorroborated crimes of your children. Where's your common sense?"

"Where's yours?"

"Damn it, if you get involved with some crack-brained scheme of Mitzi's—"

"You'll what?"

"Don't yell. Facts are facts. Mitzi would have trouble keeping her *own* child if her ex-husband got on a high horse. It's happened before. If she's not aware of how vulnerable she is, she's lost her grip on reality."

"It's outrageous!"

"I'm not saying it's hunkey-dorey. I'm saying it's a fact, so for god's sake don't egg her on."

"*I'm* egging her on?"

"Betsy, please."

"Go on then, hurry up and leave. You don't care about anything I care about!"

"Would you like to come with me?" But it was too late to ask. And besides, it was true. Betsy stood in icy silence with a scarlet face and lips pinched shut.

"You want to?" Just the same he tried again, and then said, "Jackass!" because he'd yanked clumsily on the overnight bag zipper and caught his finger in it. He sucked at the pinched place mentally calling himself jackass a few more times but it didn't do any good.

"No," she finally said.

"I'll call you."

"Sure, fine."

He walked to the door.

"Bets?"

No answer.

"You kissing me goodbye?"

"Sure, fine." She walked to him and turned up a still face. I know why wife beaters get their kicks he thought, carefully kissing her faintly freckled forehead. Then he reached behind her head and pulled a lock of hair.

"Yow!" she screeched.

Max grinned. "Keep your hair on, as they said in the Old West."

"Humph," she snorted. She shoved him over the sill and shut the door. He could hear her making noise with the locks, but he thought—or hoped—he'd seen her holding in a smile before the door blocked the space between them.

#

Something felt wrong. Max shifted down on the long curve that connected the Saw Mill Parkway to the Taconic. It was raining harder out here in Westchester—a steady featureless pour sloshing the highway and pounding the dark land beyond the lighted roadway. The wipers swished hypnotically; the motor was doing fine; the traffic was finally thinner. But a car behind was following too closely and the glare of its headlights lit the Volvo's interior making a picture of it reflect on the windshield.

The overhead lights of the Interchange ended. Max

speeded up. He should be at Robby's house by eight o'clock, he figured. Find something to eat, crash, and be ready for a long day Monday. A muscle in his shoulder cramped just slightly; he squirmed and let his thoughts drift.

He and Robby had once gone on an eight-day binge. Had it been Christmas time? The details muddled but a bright succession of faces and places floated in his head. They'd traveled from party to restaurant to bar from uptown to downtown, to apartments and lofts, in out of taxis, sleeping in snatches, singing on buses, arguing drunkenly about history and art gossip. An epic blowout. Was it really eight days? Robby had introduced him to the city's literary scene - everyone from accolade-laden critic-professor la-de-dah, with expensive canapés and a white-coated bartender, to a speed-freak post-modernist with a bathtub full of pornographic manuscripts. That son-of-a-bitch, he remembered vividly, had poured a bottle of beer on Robby's pants. It *had* been Christmas time. They'd decamped down the steep six flights of stairs and found an all-night discount store to buy him something dry. The store had been full of tinsel and candy. Robby had changed right in the aisle. And later, an impeccably dressed uptown publisher with a near-operatic voice had led his embarrassed guests in a Christmas carol sing-along in front of his fireplace.

Where had the money come from? They must have dropped plenty on cabs and drinks. Was that Robby's first advance?

"Always remember," Robby had intoned solemnly, "everyone's scared of an artist. You might be a quack or you might not and not a single one of them really knows how to tell. It's all done with mirrors. That's why sometimes it pays to be crazy."

Is that what you're doing now, friend? Max wondered. The car behind was still too close. Max slowed to let it pass. It slowed.

Max upped and lowered his lights a few times. If the driver behind noticed the okay-to-pass signal, it was ignored. He unrolled his window after a minute, sticking his arm out into the cold rain to rub and adjust his side view mirror.

"Pass, damn you," he called into the wind.

The car remained where it was. It was a little car, a sports car, black or maybe dark blue. Max peered. It was not new; it was an MG 1955 or thereabouts, a classic. Max speeded up again. It had been behind him for some time, he realized uneasily. He'd noticed it in the traffic jam along the Henry Hudson in the Bronx. He hit the horn, two shorts and a long, then blinked his lights again. The car behind dropped its high beams. Max passed an overloaded Oldsmobile. The MG followed.

"In real life," Robby had gone on, "the kid who says the emperor is naked gets taken to the child psychiatrist. If you get established as the genuine article, the people who helped you along can be ruined if a bigger fish says you're really no good. That's why it's so slow, they've all got to be cautious. Got nothing to do with your work being ahead of your time! You can't be ahead of your time unless you're from outer space, you know."

What the hell's going on? Max thought. He looked for a place to stop, an exit road to a bar, a coffee shop— anything to get this driver off his tail—but the parkway twisted through dark wooded countryside. Not even a scenic overlook offered itself. Max joined a little knot of traffic with relief. But soon the cars in the knot passed each other in turn until the clump dissolved and gaps grew wide between them. Max and the MG stuck together.

Like me and Betsy, he thought. He didn't want that thought. He didn't want to have this surge of sourness overwhelm him.

"There is nothing we can do about it!" he shouted emphatically. "We have no place for Sidney Pendergast in our lives. You can't twist us into a pretzel to make it turn out right, Betsy!" Can I twist myself to make my work do more, an interior devil suddenly demanded.

Preoccupied, he missed the turn off toward Maquaset. Fifteen minutes later, he let the turn off to Hargate Corners go by him as well, this time on purpose. He took the next exit, coming to a dead stop at the bottom of the sharp curve. The MG rolled by above, still on the parkway. Max had a pang of shame. Maybe the driver was just a sensible slob who hates driving in hard rain and had picked himself a car to follow. Max had done that himself driving a rented trailer truck full of his work on a snowy night in Massachusetts. The driver he followed had saved his ass.

Robby's Solution

The sky over the Putnam County Courthouse was high and clean; a light breeze carried the scent of cold soaked woodland and damp earth. Only last week the hills had been bleak gray, now they glowed with a faint haze of puce and purple from swelling tree buds. Lawns shone acid green. The willows by the swamp wore a cloud of Naples Yellow.

Spring really is coming. It would be right to feel in harmony with a day like this, to feel clean washed and new, but Max had tossed and twisted, stared at Robby's cardboard ceiling, and woken once with his cheeks wet with tears. To top it off, when he finally slept he overslept and Robby's Monday morning hearing had passed while he was snoring. He tried to look pleasant as he plodded across the marble foyer following a cardboard arrow labeled 'Information.'

"Can I help you, sir?" asked a young woman behind a high wooden counter. The regulations for fishing licenses were posted on the wall behind her.

"I'm looking for an officer of the court. A friend of mine was supposed to have a hearing this morning."

"Oh they're all finished now."

"Where can I find out what went on?"

"Recorder's office, second floor, third door on the left." She pointed to a curving flight of steps with an ornate iron railing. But no one was there; the door was locked. Max tried a room next door with an unlabeled door. Three middle-aged women sitting at typewriter desks looked up guiltily. One began immediately tapping her machine, another shoved belongings into a large pocketbook and shut it with a clump. The third woman took charge of Max.

"He's not there?" She had yellow dyed hair and she raised her painted eyebrows at her friends. "Well!"

The woman typing suppressed a giggle.

"Could you help me then?" Max smiled.

With an elaborate show of what a major favor she was doing by allowing herself to be persuaded she moved out of her chair and through the connecting door to the recorder's office. She held a sheaf of forms possessively in her hands when she returned.

"Rosen, Rosen," she murmured, running through them. "They've put him back upstairs, honey."

"Jail?" Max asked, putting on an innocent look.

"Ten days or two hundred dollars," she read. "Said he couldn't pay." She looked expectantly for his reaction.

"Can I see him?"

"You'll have to ask them."

"Was he represented by anyone?"

She gave him a pitying look—as if he'd asked if you can drive without gas in your car. "Kent Brinkman, he's Legal Aid." Max pried the address out of her; it was just around the corner, on Water Street.

She gave him a shrewd look as he thanked her for her help.

"He's involved in that fire, isn't he?"

"Not really. Except that a friend of his died."

The typewriter stopped clacking and all three women waited for more. Max waved jauntily and headed for the stairs. The jail took up three-quarters of the building's top floor. Here the scroll work and decorative plaster ceilings of justice and administration gave way to nineteenth-century dungeon style. Huge round bars gridded the windows. The floors were stained stone. The top floor tenants rarely stayed more than a couple of days and the staff of guards and officials periodically outnumbered them. With the Monday morning hearings over, the staff was bored. Robby was, in fact, the only item in their care who aroused anyone's interest.

A large cell on the left accommodated eight metal bunks. All but three of them were stripped, the bare thin mattresses folded half way over revealing the mean metal bands that served as springs.

Three disconsolate teenage boys stood inside. The black one stuck a hand between the rails as Max went by.

"Got a cig, man?"

"Sorry, friend. Don't smoke 'em."

Something was mumbled, followed by a burst of shared laughter.

Georgia was right; they had put Robby in the isolation cell. It measured 7 x 8, held a cot bolted to the wall, a yellowed sink with just one spigot, and a very new but seatless one-piece steel toilet. Robby was sitting on the cot writing rapidly on a yellow legal pad. Torn off sheets of paper were sorted in several piles beside him and a half-dozen balled up discards lay on the floor. There wasn't room in the cell for much else.

"Hey there," the guard said crossly, "you can't do that." Robby looked up, distracted and annoyed.

"Well, Max," he said once he'd focused. His tone was

sociable and tolerant: like what a surprise to run into you; like you're interrupting me, but since it's you, I'll stop.

"That," the guard repeated, raising his voice. "You use that paper for littering, we'll confiscate the pad."

Robby looked about him puzzled. "Litter?"

"That!" the guard yelled, pointing at the balls on the floor. "Don't get smart with me."

"I would appreciate a waste can," Robby smiled up at him with dazzling charm.

"Pick it up!" The guard meant business. Robby obeyed, unruffled. He smoothed out each sheet and made a neat new pile on his cot.

"Perhaps I can mail them to the Department of Sanitation," he said reflectively. "You know, I should have thought of that years ago. It would have changed my life."

"This guy wants to see you."

"Yes, of course," Robby answered.

The guard expected something that wasn't happening and Max watched without expression while he took out his disappointment by attacking the lock with an impressive key. He slammed the bars shut after Max stepped in and stood in the corridor glowering.

Max shook hands carefully, instead of hugging. Robby was calm and distant. The bruise on his jaw where Max had hit him had turned green and yellow.

"It's all coming together," Robby announced seriously. He pointed to the neat stacks of paper on the bunk. "I have it. A sequel to *Light Dented.* Almost!"

"How are you, Rob?"

"Me? Oh fine, fine." He looked lovingly from pile to

pile. "Food's not as good as Yaddo, but it's a lot better than some of the camps I got sent to as a kid. There *are* interruptions. It was damn noisy around here till almost morning. And they turn the lights out at midnight." He shrugged acceptingly. "There's nothing else to do but work. But another two days and I'll be ready to do a final draft of the first chapter." He shook his head with satisfaction and smiled up at Max.

"It's not over," Max said.

"What?"

"They think you're going to confess."

"Yeah," Robby laughed. "They wanted me to take a lie detector test. If I did, they'd probably toss me out of here. One thing to say for jail, Max, it's really *safe.*"

"I found your papers."

"Max!" Robby grabbed at his shoulders, his eyes suddenly hot and concerned.

"They're in the vault at Wilson Hill. Shirley left them there. No one's seen them. No one."

Robby's face relaxed into an idiot's smirk. "We we we," he said emphatically, expelling his tension. He giggled.

"Don't fool around with this, Robby."

He wrinkled his face like an aging elf. "You're so right! I'm giving it up. Dumping that book, those papers, the research, the whole damn deal. I've done a lot of thinking since Friday night—and those papers were the only things that bothered me, the only things out of my control. I had something started in *Light Dented,* you know, but I'd only scratched the surface—there's *territory* there. There's years of work—so why did I have to let myself get tied up all over again in Jewish history and all those stinking burdens that are forever, and, I fear, are so lovingly assumed by all us hopeless yids. This thing, this thing—" he waved his hand at his bunk, his face illuminated. "Max, I'm free!"

"Then for god's sake, take the lie detector test, pay the fine, and get yourself the hell out of here," Max interrupted. "As long as they think you did it, they aren't gonna find who did."

"Oh, but I can't do that."

"What are you talking about?"

"I'll break the thread if I leave. Don't you realize what this is doing for me? Half of this new book takes place in a cell. I need every minute."

"Robby, this isn't a game!"

"I agree. I'm really serious."

Max studied Robby's glowing face. He was almost always right about what was essential to him; he'd hold onto it like the fool on the Tarot card who only sees the butterfly he's about to catch and not the alligator he's stepping on.

Max tried another tack: "Heppmeyer must know where you are. It's in the papers."

"But I'm safe here, that's just the point." Robby smiled again. "I'll think about the mess with Heppmeyer when I get out. I'm free in here."

"You're playing with fire, man. It could blow up in your face. Ten days is one thing, suppose you end up in the pen for fifteen or twenty years?"

Robby looked stubborn.

"I'll get the two hundred bucks for you."

Robby shook his head.

"Don't you care who killed Shirley?"

"Do you?" Robby said.

"Damn you, yes!"

"Somebody local did it." Robby was off-hand, the matter was settled to him.

"Why do you say that? What do you know?"

"Just stands to reason, Max. Some of the locals are, well, they don't like us much."

"But just like that? Why?"

Robby looked thoughtful.

"If you're right," Max pressed, "all the more reason you're sitting on a powder keg. Don't be an asshole."

"Oh, calm down Max!"

"What's to stop someone from phoneying up some evidence against you? There's someone out there, Robby, with a powerful interest in seeing you get nailed for this because *they* did it."

The thought worried him just a little, but he wouldn't give in. He just stood there, shaking his head.

"I'll be back later, if they'll let me see you," Max said at last. "If you hadn't lived such a cotton-wool middle-class life you'd know what I'm talking about. Jesus, man, can't you believe a world of trouble is staring you right in the face?"

"You don't need to worry so," Robby said softly.

"Fuck you. Do you need anything? Soap, cigarettes?"

"Do you think they'd let me have my typewriter in here?"

"I think you're lucky they don't come in here and wring your goddamn neck. Let me out, please, officer. I've had enough."

The MG Again

The state police were in a cheerful Smokey-the-Bear mood. They smiled and called him sir. Max was a good citizen, and they, the helpful, clean-shaven guardians of the peace. Maybe it was the beautiful spring weather.

Irelli was unaffected by it; he was as weary and watery as he'd been late the previous Thursday. But then the window in his office didn't open and the only breeze he got came filtered through the fan of his air conditioner stinking of old metal and dust. He glanced wistfully through the glass and grimaced. But the coffee in his urn was fresh.

Max sat in the same green chair and outlined what he knew. Shirley's relationship with Charlene Burke, with Dick Conway, and with her brother Tyrone. Irelli knew about Rashid Ijusiri; the FBI had been trying to trace the man for several years. He took a few notes, politely, now and then looking up carefully to watch Max's face. And he was willing to answer a few questions. Yes, his men had checked local distributors of gasoline. It was ordinary white gas, the stuff sold to campers and sportsman, and in a thirty-mile radius there were more than a hundred places where it could be purchased.

"In spite of what you see on TV, clerks don't remember their customers. You got a slip of paper says three cans of gas, the guy won't remember whoop," he said. They were checking for form's sake, he continued, but no one expected a lead. He stood up and tucked his shirt down inside his belt.

"What do you know about a friend of hers named Swann?" he asked casually.

"Swann?"

"Franklin Swann. Seems he's never called Frank. He's some kind of artist."

Max pulled at his beard. "I know I've heard of him," he muttered mostly to himself, "Swann, Swann—he's a sculptor, yeah. He had a show in Soho last year. The Raw Fish Gallery." Max remembered: constructions with feathers and sticks, rocks woven together with ropes. In fact, he'd had an argument about the work with Betsy. She'd said it was very sensitive. Max thought it was trash.

"Does he live up here?" Max asked.

"Not far." Irelli shuffled through a folder. "Phone company's got a record of a call from the Pendergast number to his at 5:37 Wednesday afternoon. It's a toll call. It didn't go over three minutes. It was the only call that day."

"Have you spoken to him?"

"We think we got a love triangle here, Mr. Birtwhistle. Happens to smart dames like that. She slept with one man too many."

"Did you know about Conway before I came in here?"

Irelli smiled. "We spoke to him."

"He doesn't seem the type," Max said, feeling foolish.

"Type, what's the type?" Irelli responded wearily. "Smart dame, sleeping around. But Conway didn't leave New York. We checked out his garage."

"Trains, taxi-cabs?" Max offered.

"Look we know who was using the taxis. Six o'clock Thursday morning, your pal Rosen was in a cab to

Peekskill, screaming like a lunatic. Couldn't leave town fast enough."

Max shook his head.

"Look," Irelli outlined patiently, "the M.E. spells it out. The victim was hit sixteen eighteen times. That spells what you call passion."

"Have you checked Robby's car? It's probably still out on Horse Creek Road."

"We've got the car. We're working on it."

Max suppressed a pang of fear.

"So you didn't know about Pendergast and this Swan fellow?" Irelli pressed.

"Someone did say she had a boy friend up here," Max admitted. "She kept it very quiet."

"Not so quiet as you didn't hear anything."

"The friend who mentioned it didn't even know his name."

"And who was that?"

Max told him about Glazer and provided his address and telephone number. Irelli added it to the notebook where he'd listed all the others.

"Okay, thank you for coming in this way. We appreciate it. But take a little advice from me—if you hear anything else, you tell me. Don't go poking around yourself, it'll get ya in trouble."

The interview was over; Max stood up.

"Her brother Tyrone's the one who worries me the most. His van might be registered in West Virginia. He lived there somewhere before he moved to Baltimore," Max said from the door.

"We'll check it."

"And you might find Swann through his gallery. Raw Fish. The woman who runs it is Edith, spelled with a y."

Irelli nodded.

"Where did you say Swann lived?"

"Up here." He wasn't going to say more. His eyes were pitying. It was pity for him, Max realized uncomfortably, the trusting friend— the schnook who'd sooner or later have to face some ugly facts about the man in the local jail.

#

Swann, now that got under Max's skin. From a phone at the gas station across the street, Max telephoned Raw Fish.

"Sorry, we're not open today," said Edyth with a y. Max rambled on, more or less, and she finally eased up and provided Franklin's phone number. Max listened to it ring until his ear was tired of the pressure of the receiver. He was thinking more than listening, and thinking even more intently as he walked to his car.

There were two ways to approach this: to look at the facts at hand—the day, the time, the things: hammer and gas cans (the method); establish who could have known where Shirley was that day (the opportunity) and from that derive a motive. The other way was the wide lens, to look at her life, the whole of the scene the way you'd look at a painting. Where did it move? Where were the shapes that had led to a passionate murder? Like a painting, he mused, steering his car onto the cross-county road.

But the people in her life were also central figures in their own pictures. If Tyrone makes a shape in Shirley's pattern, Shirley also makes one in his. Most of the patterns are half-known, in shadow. Relationships between them are shadows on top of shadows. Suppose the murder, so central in Shirley's story—the raw, broken ending of her life—was a peripheral occurrence in the life-scene of the murderer? Patterns can overlap or they can touch only on one small but deadly spot.

No wonder the police stick to the first way: checking the objects—dried blood, train timetables, fingerprints. And yet Irelli, professional policeman that he was, wasn't checking facts objectively. He'd begun to spin himself his own story: "Smart dame like that." "One man too many."

Max stopped behind a yellow school bus disgorging children. He was surprised, it didn't seem late enough for school to be out. The sun was bright and high and the light still almost morning-clear.

Several children, released, tore across a meadow toward a group of houses back from the road. Two boys fell into the dry roadside weeds, a squirming heap. They wrestled gleefully while kids inside the bus squealed at them through the bus windows. There'd be no way to pass, Max thought impatiently; he checked his rearview. Over the hillcrest behind him, a dark green sports car appeared. It was an MG, 1955.

Max put his head out of the window for a better look. The bus released diesel farts and began to roll ahead. Max eased into first. Glazer and Swann, Swann and Conway. Could it have been that simple? Irelli had put it flatly: "One man too many."

Repressed, dutiful Glazer, the friend who had never been a lover, watching his beloved bed man after man.

A classic story; it's a classic because it does happen that way. Max remembered Glazer's shaking fingers, the way his eyes had roved painfully over the rooftops while they stood together at Lynn and Mitzi's window.

The school bus stopped again; this time the MG was right behind him but sun glared on its windshield and Max couldn't see the driver. It was the same car, though, Max was sure. He shook himself. Why had Glazer approached him? He studied the MG again. Am I too suspicious in one place and not enough in another? Glazer hadn't sounded any false notes; he seemed to be exactly what he seemed to be, a man who needed to talk to someone, anyone, about how shattered he felt, about how much he cared. Max went over their conversation in his mind.

Who the hell is in this goddamn MG? He ground the Volvo's gears by downshifting too violently as the bus again flapped out its metal stop sign. Temper, temper, he ordered himself, control yourself.

This time Max could make out a blond head, a male, in the MG's driver's seat. A row of kids in the back window of the bus were making faces. Max looked up at them thoughtfully and responded by miming donkey ears. They surged to the window glass, screaming with soundless laughter, pointing down at him. He crossed his eyes and bared his teeth. The back window packed with faces. One of them held up a notebook, but Max couldn't make out what was drawn or written on the bobbing page.

Abruptly they withdrew, all the heads disappearing, and Max, without hearing it, knew the driver must be yelling threats. An atmosphere of chastisement and suppressed excitement vibrated out of the yellow sides. The bus bumbled slowly up to a cross road, then lurched carefully left with signal light blinking and a long, pointing arm protruding from the driver's side. Heads popped up again as the bus turned away. A little girl waved.

The MG stayed with Max. It was eaten by rust along the bottom and the fenders were crinkled and daubed with black car dope. It followed persistently, just as it had last night. Max wanted out. He was sweating in the cool wind; the winding, dipping country road was making him feel faintly queasy. What a sailor I am! I was all over the South Atlantic in an oil tanker and here I'm getting seasick on a goddamn country road.

He bore right toward Hargate Corners, taking the route that would lead him to the bar. He was driving fast now, so fast that his turn into the bar's parking lot sprayed a noisy arc of gravel. He stopped, backed swiftly to rest by a railroad tie, and watched the dark green MG continue on.

"Damn funny twice in twenty-four hours," he said out loud. The MG's back end carried an ordinary New York State license plate.

#

Dark, quiet, stale—the bar was a haven. Sunlight at the red painted windows made a few squares of ruby light on the dark brown floor. Two men at the bar's far end drank beers comfortably. The bartender wasn't the same man Max had seen before but there was a resemblance that suggested family around his nose and eyes and in the way he held his shoulders.

"I'm his son," the barkeep explained affably, bringing Max a cold draft. It was quiet enough for Max to hear the eggs he ordered snapping on the grill in the kitchen. They came on a platter with thick fresh home fries.

"Fishing don't begin until next Friday," he remarked clearly fishing himself.

"Never was much for fishing," Max answered. "City boy, I guess."

"You from New York?"

"Detroit originally. I'm staying with a friend a couple a days." The bartender was young. Max smiled. "Got some thinking to do."

The bartender grinned boyishly.

"Yeah, Deeetroits," Max continued nostalgically, "seems like I spent my whole life there up to my armpits in a motor. First car I ever had I put together myself out of parts."

"Oh yeah?" the boy looked interested.

"It had a Studebaker engine. You probably don't remember them. Best engine in the country in the late forties. A Chevvy frame..." The front door opened and the bartender looked up.

"Hey, Ray, come over here, you oughta listen to this guy."

A man in a white jump suit loped across the floor toward them. He was the stutterer Max had seen on Thursday evening. He smiled in a tired, distracted way, put up one finger for his order, and took a stool next to Max.

"Hey," he said, acknowledging Max with a laconic nod.

"This guy custom built his car from scratch," the barkeep repeated.

"Max," Max said sociably.

"Max is it?" The boy stuck his hand across the bar. "I'm Jimmy, this is Ray."

"C..c..can't forget it," Ray smiled, pointing to the name in dark blue embroidery on his pocket.

"I still have a picture of it," Max said, feeling a little silly. My first love, he didn't say while he fumbled through his wallet. It was stuck behind an expired library card. He passed it over—a faded color snapshot of the Birtmobile under a tree at Belle Isle park. There weren't any people in the picture but Max remembered the day vividly, who was with him, what they'd done. He wished he hadn't brought the subject up at all because he knew very well he'd have to follow it up with predictable banalities, until the two men with him were bored. It was not the way he wanted to talk about that car or those times. He swallowed down the sense of self-betrayal and responded to what they asked.

Ray's questions were brief and technical. Jimmy's more romantic.

"You still have it?" Jimmy wanted to know.

"Christ, no," Max jerked his thumb toward the front door. "I drive a Volvo now, and I don't even fix it myself."

"Good machine a c..c..c couple a years ago. Getting shitty now," Ray offered.

"I heard that," Max agreed. "You get a lot of foreign cars up here?"

"They go down Westchester for s..s.. servicing. I mean the c..c..lassy ones... T..too bad," He looked at his large hands self-consciously.

"You're good at it," Max said.

Ray blushed, jammed one hand in his pocket and grabbed for his beer with the other. "I got a '72 BMW up on blocks in the back, bought it off a junker three years ago for t...t...t...two hundred bucks. That's how b..bad it was." He nodded his head. "I'm gettin' there."

"You ever fix a 55 MG, dark green? Two times the guy who's driving it has damn near rear-ended me. Right up the road."

"I've seen that car," Jimmy said.

"He don't live here," Ray said reflectively. "I think he was—" He stopped abruptly. He pulled a few bills out of his billfold, plopped them on the bar and walked out.

Jimmy looked stunned, then, conscious of Max's surprise, took the money to the register, rang it up, and busied himself dusting bottles that weren't dirty on the other side of the kitchen pass-through. Max watched quietly, finishing his beer. He paid Jimmy without comment, got change for the phone, and called Swann again. This time the ring was answered.

The sun was setting and Max drove west into it. He was to look for a private road, and a mock-medieval stone gateway with 'Kingswood' in gothic letters on its arch. You couldn't miss it, Swann had assured him over the phone. He'd known Max's name but hadn't seemed happy about the idea that Max was dropping by. Max said only that Edyth had given him the number.

The countryside was less thickly wooded as he turned north. The road bumped and wound through farmland along the Hudson River, following its course but not closely enough to impinge on the great riverside estates. They stretched from the Bronx to Albany, the feudal kingdoms of Dutch noblemen, the New World plantations of English gentry, the playgrounds and retreats of Gilded Age merchant princes. The rich no matter who they are always know where the beautiful land is, Max thought. Not very long ago, one of these places had been a center for quasi-religious drug tripping; another was presently the home of an Eastern religious group with a sinister reputation for brainwashing and kidnap. Some were communes and some corporate conference centers, and some remained what they had always been, private properties for the super-rich.

He caught a glimpse of the river; it reflected the pinkening sky as purely as the Hudson Valley painters had represented it a hundred years ago. The river wasn't clean back then either. People tossed dead horses in it, apple cores, pig manure, human sewage—and downstream people sickened of cholera and typhoid fever. Today it's industrial wastes, chemicals of unknown composition, and people sicken of cancer and craziness.

Max found the medieval arch, turned under it, and followed a yellow concrete drive. The spires of the house were sun-struck and all its western windows were glittering gold. Max slowed down shaking his head reflexively. The joint was a monstrosity—part Swiss chalet, part gothic castle, part Victorian country house with gingerbread. Long flowerbeds all neatly mulched sloped down the hill toward the view of distant mountains across the river. The littlest crocuses had already started opening, showing white and gold in low orderly flanks along the outside edges. The lawns were evenly mowed, the house trim smartly painted. The big house was unoccupied Swann had told him. He lived in the carriage barn, the one painted green.

The drive took Max behind the house to a wide turnaround facing a six-door garage and two nondescript outbuildings. Neither was green but a dark green MG was drawn up by one of the garage doors. The now well-known body was dented and rust-eaten with black dope mottled fenders. Max parked beside it.

"Swann!" he hollered. Some chimney swallows circled in the air above the house. He walked past the second outbuilding following a two-track dirt road up a rise. After the crest a green barn appeared, half-circled by enormous pine trees. It had a row of skylights and a modern picture window cut into its side. Swann was sitting on a bench in front, watching Max walk toward him. Or he seemed to be watching but he didn't move.

"Swann?" Max shouted again.

The man jumped up with a start and half-jogged down the road to his visitor. "You gotta bear with me, man. I'm kinda flakey today," he said extending his hand and putting out boyish charm for Max to admire.

He was large and young. Sun-bleached blond hair was thick on his tanned arms and at the neck of his pink tee shirt. His shoulders were muscular. He clearly expected people to respond to him pleasantly—he was young American manhood, well-developed, self-assured. Except a deep worry line divided his hazel eyes, and one of them was larger than the other. His long nose bent sharply to one side so his face looked as if it had been folded in half and then smoothed out and spread flat again.

Max decided not to fool around: "Have you heard from the state police?"

Swann's face twitched with shock. He almost looked dumb. "They woke me up this morning, man. I didn't know a thing about it. Are you talking about Shirley?" Suspicion clouded his eyes and he glanced around, letting Max know he was suddenly conscious of being all alone.

Max nodded. "You know you've tailed me twice in the past day Swann."

"Tailed you?"

"I drive a light blue Volvo. All the way out here from the Hudson River Drive last night, all the way to Hargate Corners from Maquaset this afternoon. I figured you must want to meet me."

"Oh, Jesus." He ran his hands through his well-cut hair. It was balding just a little at the front. "Max, believe me, I didn't even *see* you this afternoon. I don't know where I was. The cops woke me up this morning and told me Shirl was dead. I mean I raced over there. I was so numb it didn't hit me till they were finished talking to me, you know what I mean? I went to get a cup of coffee and I'm sitting at a fucking *lunch* counter, crying my eyes out, you know. Everybody looking at me. Jesus! I mean I really wasn't following you."

"Hey," Max said. He put a hand on Franklin's bulging upper arm and gave his bicep a reassuring squeeze.

"Look, come on up" Swann said.

"What about last night?" Max pressed.

"I do that sometimes," he admitted, "follow when I'm really tired."

"What?"

"Follow a good driver," he shook his head ruefully. "I guess it's pretty shitty." He raised his eyebrows and looked shrewd. "I follow the guys with the CB antennas all the time. I figure they'll know where the speed traps are."

He led Max around the corner of the barn and through a storm door. It was a class-A studio. The old barn flooring had been scraped and bleached. Expensive lighting fixtures of chrome and stainless steel lit the wide interior. Shiny power tools rested on pine workbenches among the heaps of stuff Swann used: pebbles, feathers, aging rope, weathered branches. There was a modern wood lathe standing by one wall but no scent of wood dust, no acrid tang of glue compounds. Clearly Swann hadn't worked in a while.

Max followed him up the steps to his living quarters in the loft.

"Wow," Max breathed.

"Something, isn't it?" Swann agreed.

Max stood at the loft railing looking down over the workspace and directly out through the high picture window. The pasture slid down to the mansion, now a softly greying jigsaw shape. The lawns beyond had turned dark blue all the way to the black trees but the river beyond them was wide and clear and shining like a sheet of pewter. Way across the river, mountain shapes cut against the still faintly colored sky.

"I don't think I'd paint," Max said after a while. "I'd just sit here."

"It's good for me, man, I need it," Swann said. He went to the sink, shoved at some dirty dishes and began to fill a kettle.

"If you want a joint, the stuff's on the table," he said. Max sat down. The bed was rumpled and slept in. An open suitcase on the floor was full of disorderly clothing.

"Is this your. . ."

"What the fuck's going. . .

They'd both spoken at the same time.

"What the fuck's going on?" Swann repeated. "Shirley was *murdered?* Who'd kill her? They thought I did!" He slammed his arms down against his thighs. "Man, I don't know which way is up. How do you fit into this?" he asked belligerently, to cover his surging uneasiness. "You a friend of hers?"

"Not close, but yeah for years," Max said. "I was at home in the city. They've checked me out too."

"They asked me a lot of questions about some friend of hers named Rosen. They've got him locked up."

"He's a friend of mine too, he has a house near Hargate. They're way off base. He was worried about some papers he thought she had, so he tried to get into her house after the fire was out."

"This is a nightmare," Franklin moved closer to Max, the fold between his eyes deeply creased. He was not sure what to trust. "What are they up to? I slept with Shirley a couple of times. It gets lonely up there. But I don't care what she did with anyone else. None of my business. I wouldn't kill her. Jesus!"

"Do they still think you did?" Max asked.

"I've got an alibi. How's that for shit. I was eating dinner with the Ockburgh's. Then we all flew down to Washington. That's where I've been. Helen wanted to see the show at the Hirshhorn."

"The Ockburgh's?"

"They own this place. Used to belong to Walter's father. Man, I'd have been at Shirley's place Wednesday night if they hadn't been so hot to go early. Jesus shit!"

The kettle boiled and Franklin made a pot of red zinger tea. He slouched in the chair next to Max and began spooning honey into his cup. Max let the cup he'd been given sit untouched on the table. He disliked herb teas.

"Don't you want some dope?" Franklin asked, making jabbing motions with his dripping spoon at cigarette papers and a glass jar in the middle of the table.

"Don't feel much like it," Max answered.

"Me neither. I feel like getting blind ass drunk." He jammed the spoon into his cup and headed for the icebox. He returned with two smudgy glasses and a bottle of ten-year-old scotch. The scotch was icy cold.

"Helen gave me this for Christmas. I don't drink much. Man, the Ockburgh's! I better talk to them. They'll be having a fit." He gulped at his glass, refilled it, added more to Max's and sprawled on his bed with the telephone.

Max sipped slowly, taking it in.

"Walter? It's me... No, thanks, I'm all right. I should have called you sooner... Yeah, she's the one, a friend of mine... I feel sick... No, they don't. There's no reason why anybody would, she was a nice person...Yeah, burned it down... I know I told you so, and I really think you should... Okay, I'll call them tomorrow. And, look I'm sorry they bothered you that way... Thanks, and please give my love to Helen."

"They're really very nice," Franklin said, untangling himself from the long telephone cord and sitting up. "They fixed this place for me, they've been fantastic."

"You work for them?"

"Well, yes and no. It's sort of—they've bought some work of mine. Helen really likes my work. And see, they don't live here much except in the summer and there's a lot of trouble around here. You know, kids breaking in. Some of it's been real ugly. The fact is, some of it isn't kids. There's been some professional thieving. So, you know, I was having a little trouble with my landlord, and the city was really interfering with my head—so we worked it out for me to live here. Now the locals know the place is occupied —." He looked around his domain and swallowed away at his scotch. "They're really great people, man, really hip. Helen studied painting with

Hans Hoffman. She knew everybody in Provincetown in the fifties. Musta been wild. She tells some unbelievable stories. You ever hear of her? Her name was Helen Steinway before she married Walter. Doesn't paint anymore though."

Max shook his head.

"They're having a fit," he continued. "See, I told 'em I thought they ought to have a wired gate. Even with me here."

The phone rang sharply, as if in response to this.

"Helen, dear... Yeah, believe me I *really* am... Hargate Corners. It's about fifteen miles from here... I don't think we need to... Really, Helen, I think it would be a nuisance. I. . . . Well, okay if you think so." Franklin made a face and pointed at the phone. "Okay...okay ... Don't worry, Helen, I'll call. And thanks. Really. Jesus." He put the phone down on the floor between his legs and looked at it.

She wants me to get a Doberman Pinscher. They're really shook up." He shook his head. "Ja know Shirley long?"

About fifteen years."

"I didn't know any of her friends. Not even your guy, the one in jail. I met her last summer in a parking lot. She couldn't get her car to start. It's weird, man. I hardly know anything about her. I didn't even have her home phone number in New York, just her office."

"I wish you knew something," Max said. He put his hand on top of his empty glass to stop Franklin from adding more. "When was the last time you saw her?"

"Yeah, the cops asked that. We figured it out. March

8th. She'd been up here for a long weekend at the beginning of the month—but she was with her kid then so I didn't see her. She came back the 8th. We had supper that night."

"What did you talk about?"

"Oh, man, you know. I was pretty horny." Franklin's eyes were glazing. The worry line deepened in his flushed face. "Man, I feel weirded out. All I remember is fucking her. That's the truth."

"You'll get the rest," Max said gently. "Look I'm staying at Rosen's house. I'll call you tomorrow—"

"Don't go!"

"Another few more belts and you're gonna be snoring," Max answered.

"I'd just as soon not—not do any thinking tonight." Franklin paced around the table, bottle in one hand, glass in the other. "I've been babbling, haven't I?"

Max didn't answer. "How'd you become a sculptor, Franklin?" he asked to break the long silence.

"I went to school," he said. "Berkeley's a real good school." The phone rang. Franklin jumped. It was Helen Ockburgh again.

"I'm just a little drunk, Helen," he explained into the phone. "Don't worry... Sure, sure I'll do it for you. I don't think its silly... The porch lights too?...No, I don't," he burst out emotionally, "I love it when you baby me. I'll turn them on right now. I'm going now. Bye."

He dropped the receiver clumsily into the cradle and sank into the pillows. His eyes were open but Max thought he'd passed out. He was quiet for so long Max leaned over the bed to loosen his belt and open up his shirt.

"She wants me to turn the lights on in the big house,"

Franklin whispered. "She's afraid some crazy arsonist is coming to burn me next. Because I was sleeping with Shirl. Walter's furious she's making such a fuss..."

He struggled to sit up. "I think I'm supposed to fuck her, but I'm really scared. Suppose Walter—I've got such a good deal here. This studio's heaven. I'm bisexual," he announced abruptly.

"Maybe you're supposed to make it with both of them."

"Oh you don't know Walter," he said seriously. Franklin struggled to his feet:

"Stay with me, Max. You won't be sorry, I promise you."

"Take it easy. You're gonna be all right." Max handed him his glass of whiskey and started down the loft steps.

"Please," Franklin said miserably. "You won't be sorry."

"I'll talk to you later. Get some sleep, okay?"

Back at the Bar Again

Max pulled into the parking lot of the red-windowed bar; the turn was beginning to feel familiar and he wondered idly if the place had a name or if it too was simply "the bar" for its regular patrons.

It had been a long time since that had happened to him. He had twinges of sympathy as physical as muscle pangs for Franklin, for Shirley, for anyone who craved a bed-mate on a scary, lonely night. At the same time he felt imposed on and his annoyance was as sharp as his sympathy.

It was past ten on the neon-ringed bar clock. He wondered where Betsy was. The clientele was, as before, all male. Jimmy's father Jim was back on duty and Ray sat at the bar with another man, apart from the group watching spring training on the blurry black and white TV. The sound was turned very low and the fans were supplying their own sporadic commentary. The game wasn't pleasing them. Max half-expected to see his father's tired face at the table. He'd have been in the middle all right, drawling out some scurrilous remark. His years in Detroit and his German-American wife never caused him to lose his red-dirt East Tennessee twang.

Max took a stool one over from Ray's and asked for a bourbon. When he got it, he gestured up with the glass and nodded at the two men. Ray looked uncomfortable. His companion looked up, first at Max, then back at Ray.

"Who's your friend?" he asked Ray. He had flaccid unhealthy looking jowls, a soft belly, and drooping shoulders. His greying hair was pushed straight back and there were grey pouches under his pale eyes. He looked like a heart attack about to happen, down to the filter cigarette he clutched tensely between two clubbed tobacco-yellowed fingertips.

Ray shrugged and rubbed a hand across his hair boyishly.

"I was in here a couple of minutes this afternoon," Max told him, "talking to Ray about my car building days."

Ray scraped his stool back and loped to the door marked "Gents."

"He's not one of your long-distance talkers," the friend offered, "but I'll tell you this. That man is an artist when it comes to cars, an artist."

"You two old friends?"

"All our lives," he began. "Ray and me. . ." The bar door opened and a heavy voice demanded "Hey, Len-boy!"

The man's shoulders rose, his mouth tightened, and he seemed to prepare himself for something as he half-turned on his stool and stuck a hand out in greeting.

"Come over here," the newcomer rasped, seating himself assertively at an empty table. He was the one the men had called Sharkey Max remembered from last Thursday night. Without being asked, the bartender drew a beer and set it at the edge of the bar. Len didn't get up as bidden, at least it seemed to Max he didn't intend to. He cleared his throat and dragged deeply on his cigarette. But when Sharkey ambled to the bar, picked up his glass, and jerked his large arm in a come gesture,

Len let himself slide off the stool and move slowly to the table. He moved painfully, he was almost shuffling.

"Gotta keep you from contamination," Sharkey said loudly. The bartender stopped moving and several heads turned from the TV set to look at Max. Ray came out of the bathroom door.

"Get your glass, Ray," Sharkey boomed.

"Ss.. ss...see you," Ray mumbled, picking it up and keeping his face turned away from Max's eyes. His cheeks and neck turned mottled red.

Jim the bartender wiped at the wet rings on Max's right. "Don't mind him, fella," he said appeasingly. "Sharkey's got a bad mouth."

"What's that you said?" Sharkey asked from across the room.

"I said we're used to you. I don't know why," he was answered. There was an edge in the old bartender's voice.

"Yeah? Well, Jim, we don't need no kikey long hairs in here. Give your place a bad name."

"This place has my name, Sharkey. You got a beef with me?" He leaned out on two outstretched arms braced on the bar's lip. There was no reply. "Sheesh." the bartender concluded. He wiped the bar top over again, and then proceeded down its whole length, cleaning out unnecessarily, each of its half dozen ashtrays.

"No offense?" he asked Max when he was finished. Talking in the room had resumed. The TV had talking heads analyzing the ball game.

Max pushed his glass forward in response. "I'll have another."

"On the house."

Now a ball player was being interviewed. People at the tables near the set separated. Two or three of the watchers took the vacant stools at the bar.

"If those s.o.b.'s don't get it together bettern that, I'm gonna pack it in," one of them said with a jerk of his thumb at the TV. "Bunch a clowns!"

"Some clowns," the bartender answered. "This whole town could run a week on what one or two of them got paid today."

"Things tough around here?" Max asked.

"Ah, who can figure it out?" one of them answered. He could have been forty—or sixty. He had a hard, seamed little face and the tight, competent body of a man who has worked with his hands all his life and sleeps well at night. "I make more money a week than my dad made in two-three months. My dad raised six kids on that. We had what we needed. We didn't feel bad. Now me, I'm just barely keeping ahead of the bills, know what I mean?"

"You got a lot to crab about, R.T." His friend had heard these complaints before. He turned to Max. "All his dad ever had was a broken-down old apple farm. R.T.'s kid graduated high school last spring and he *gave* him a brand new car. That's how much he's hurting."

R.T.'s face creased up inscrutably. He spread his gnarled fingers out on the bar and watched them tap. "Yeah," he said to no one in particular, "pretty little car alright." He curled the fingers into a loose fist. "I don't know though, my boy has. . . . Things are different now, things have really changed."

He gave Max a piercing troubled look. "You got any kids?" he asked.

Max shook his head.

He was disappointed. What he wanted to say couldn't be said to an uncomprehending escapee from the nets of fatherhood. "Things really have changed." He swished his beer efficiently, downing it while beer still circled the inside of the glass.

Max adjusted his head just slightly to examine the table where Sharkey presided. Sharkey slouched with his elbows out as if to circle the table with his shoulders; he leaned forward but he wasn't speaking. His jaws moved methodically mashing up the corn chips he brought up by handfuls from the bowl below his chin. Ray traced circles with his finger on the Formica table top as intent as a child; but his face was still flushed and uncomfortable. Len caught Max's eye and turned immediately to the new cigarette he was lighting from the butt of his old one. He said something to Ray and whatever it was roused them all to conversation. They leaned together and kept their voices low.

There was a burst of laughter from another table and some bantering as one of its occupants announced his need to go home. Max thought that might be a good idea for him too, and thinking of it, ordered a beer instead. R.J. and his friend were in a similar state of mind. They talked together about baseball; they talked about cars; and R.J.'s friend ribbed him about his plumbing business, pointing out how many people he had working for him these days and suggesting he ought to stop describing himself as a working stiff. It was a sore point. R.J. was embarrassed. He responded with his trusty refrain: nothing was like it used to be. It had changed. They had changed. Everything had changed.

Boredom trickled down Max's shoulders and settled in his stomach. Unwillingly he began examining his motives for sitting there and listening to these men. They weren't particularly pleasant motives. Self-pity led the pack, and loneliness. They were the same things that chased his fellow patrons in here—and they'd be shocked if they knew that, their idea of an artist's life being what they probably were. Not the least of the sad barking dogs in his head was irresponsibility. He knew he was postponing a telephone call to Betsy. Or did he, he wondered, have something to learn here about Shirley's death? He looked quizzically toward Sharkey's table again and caught, full face, Sharkey's cold baleful glare. It was like a bolt of current; it hooked into him for a moment; he froze.

R.J. tapped Max's forearm for attention. "I'll tell you what I mean," he said, "when it comes to change. You see that fella back there?" He indicated Sharkey with a discrete shrug. "I known that guy all my life. Knew his folks too. He was one wild kid, drinking like the world would end, and running up and down on one of them big Harley cycles. Wasn't anything he wouldn't do, but I never thought of him as mean. When his dad got sick he took over the construction company. I figured he'd do all right. Everybody did. Somewhere along the line the sport just went right out of him. Same job, same town, people he's known all his life. Still had time to ride his cycle. People around here don't seem to see it, they're all used to him. But I learned a lot my ten years in the navy and I don't laugh at Sharkey Pierce. He goes on gettin' meaner every year and there's no sense to it."

"You always make a big thing out of nothing," the other man interjected placidly. "So he got older. What do you expect? I ain't what I was twenty years ago myself. To hear you talk, the world's goin to hell cause some guys are tough. Sharkey's always had a mean streak."

"See what I mean?" R. T. went on, "They just don't see it like I do."

"Aw, dry up," the friend responded mildly.

"What do you see?" Max asked.

"That's what I'm saying. Who can figure it?" Like a trick of time-lapse photography, Max saw R.T.'s face age into stubborn senility—a man played false by the certainty of his view of the world. He was stuck. Max turned up his glass to drain the last of it.

Robby, he thought with a flash of irony, would never, never drink in a place like this. He'd be terrified of being misunderstood and of misunderstanding. He would label the bar's patrons "tough" or "redneck" and he'd be in fear of humiliation, fist fights, physical pain—not this choking kinship with frightened, unreflecting men.

Hot beery breath hit the back of Max's ear. "You needa get a few things straight," Sharkey was right behind him, breathing hard.

"Lay off, Pierce," the bartender announced, affecting weariness. He wiped his hands on his towel and stuck the towel on a hook. Max set his empty glass down and got up slowly. His hands were up but loose; he leaned his back against the edge of the bar top. He didn't answer.

The man in front of him appeared almost top heavy with belligerence. Beads of sweat stood out in the dark hairs along his forehead and quivered in the thick folds of his neck. Max glanced down. Sharkey's *feet*, even in boots, were tiny, almost delicate. A quick stomp on the toes might work. Steel tipped boots? His eyes went back to the man's face to watch for the tensing in his neck that would telegraph a sudden move.

"I'm listening," Max said.

"Aw Sharkey, he's not bothering anybody," R.T.'s friend interceded apologetically.

"He oughta bother you. He's mixed up with that babe that got killed on Horse Creek Road."

The man's placid face took on a flattened look. He eyed Max hastily for a denial, then moved back a couple of steps to be neither pro or con whatever might be about to happen.

Sharkey stepped in to his advantage. "We don't need you hanging around here," he said hoarsely. It was a touch theatrical.

R.J. stood up. The top of his head was level with Sharkey's collarbone. "Butt out." he said briefly. Sharkey lurched, just slightly, and shook a meaty finger over R.J.'s head toward the bartender.

"I'm telling you, Jim, I've had dealings with these creeps!"

"Come again?" said Max.

A TV toothpaste commercial played faintly in the silence.

"You want to cool off now?" Max asked. "I don't like you."

"Oooooh eee," Sharkey whooped. It was *his* mimicry of laughter. "Ray, Len, Dave, listen to this. He don't like me." The whooping trailed off into grunts. Sharkey scanned the room with dirty eyes. This was his turf but the support he expected was missing. Men stirred, but only to make sure their views weren't obstructed. Len and Ray simply sat in their chairs.

Max didn't wait for Sharkey to gather himself. "No I don't like you. I'm quietly drinking a beer, talking with these guys. You barged in and said you had a problem. I said I'd listen. So what's the problem?"

"Here's a top off, Sharkey," the bartender set out a fresh mug of beer. It was the wrong moment for a placating gesture. Adrenalin rushed through Max's belly; his hands got cold and damp; and the big man snatched the glass and dumped it on the bar.

"You dumb sucker—when I say creep that's what I mean. Last Wednesday night old Howard Anderson's shack got burned down to the ground, you know. That Pendergast broad, don't nobody know what she was up to up there but I'll tell you this, there ain't a woman in Hargate ain't scared half crazy about what's goin' on. Your wife, Jim, and yours, and yours." He swung his arm out in a half-circle gesture, "You sit here like a bunch of clucks with *this* guy? They got his pal in jail already. What's he in here for? Well I'm man enough to tell him to get the fuck out! Fuckin city deadbeat. You know what I'm saying, R.T.? You want your old lady raped and burned?"

The bartender grabbed Max's shoulder from behind, hard: "No funny stuff inside my bar," he ordered. He wasn't sure if Max was about to throw a punch—or if he could stop the explosion that might happen if he did.

"Can you two handle this?" he asked Len and Ray, and to the face in the pass-through kitchen window he made a short gesture with his finger. The face disappeared. The cops, no, the cop, Max flashed. The fragile old crank in the shiny uniform.

"Handle it!" Sharkey roared. "There's one way." He made a marred attempt to grab for Max's shoulder and belt. Max wrenched free of him and Jim and managed to stamp down hard on Sharkey's foot. The pushing and shoving that followed—for all the heaviness of limbs and the rank adult smells of the bodies involved—reminded Max of a grammar school playground fight. But there was a bit of method in it. They wanted him outside. No one throws punches in Jim's bar. A gang coalesced that maneuvered Sharkey to a table at the farthest corner of the room, its members loudly agreeing and disagreeing with Sharkey and each other. Each had a personal interpretation he would stick to, a conclusion he'd refuse to give up, but they acted as a unit to preserve the rules of their place.

Max straightened his clothes and tried to pay for his drinks. He was gestured to forget it. He touched his forehead to R.T., the only person still sitting at the bar, and was starting up his Volvo in the parking lot when a county police car turned in.

He idled his motor a moment, watching. The bartender came to the door with what could only be a couple of six-packs in a brown paper bag. As Max drove away they were still talking at the door and the bag had passed into the officer's hands.

Max and Betsy on the Phone

The phone in Robby's hallway rang steadily from the time Max parked in the pot-holed driveway, fumbled with the lock, groped for the light switch, and dove for the receiver. Dial tone only. He slammed the thing down and cursed. He stumped into the kitchen and surveyed the mess he hadn't touched the previous night. It would have to have been Betsy, he thought, gingerly plucking a glass from the crudded pile in the sink and washing it out. He poured a fat finger of bourbon into the bottom of it and tossed it down.

"Face it, Max, you hate having to apologize," he said to himself. He sat by the phone and dialed home. Of course it had been Betsy. She was crisp. She was also, obviously, worried—about him and even about Robby. She was nonplussed when he tried to explain that Robby was staying in jail on purpose.

"It's probably the best place for him, Bets. Three meals a day and they keep him out of mischief," he said, carefully not mentioning any of the risks Robby was blithely ignoring.

"He must be nuts, Max. He might lose his job because of this."

"I don't think so. Robby pulls in a lot of students."

"I think you're nuts too," she mumbled.

"Bets, are you crying?"

"No. Of course not. Why would I cry? You're up there running around like some tin-pot saint. The cops think Robby did it so they aren't even looking anymore. And whoever did it probably knows who *you* are by now. Of course *I'm* not worried. Not good old Betsy. Stiff upper lip Betsy. I know you're not telling me one half of what you know!"

She was crying openly now and strangling a little as she spilled her words out.

"Sweetie..."

"Shit head!" He could hear her blowing her nose. "Speaking of losing jobs," she began, rapidly, before he could speak again, "this has been some Monday." Art council funds for her pottery workshop were being reduced, again, she'd been told this afternoon, and this time the director was really worried. Unless he could persuade the Y's board to make up the shortfall from their operating budget, which he doubted, the classes would end in May and not resume next fall. Betsy had had to promise to give him a detailed report: thumbnail sketches of all her students, notes on their attendance and their progress, which would take a couple of days to put together and for which, naturally, she'd get no extra pay. The director said he needed it for ammunition.

"... and it won't do him any good. I haven't got enough minority people to impress the council. Three blacks and a Puerto Rican out of a class of fourteen. I know that's all they're looking for—numbers."

"You've been there two years," Max temporized. "You'll be able to get something better."

"You don't understand again. I've got a terrific class here. Kate Sherman's stuff is getting really beautiful and it's the first thing in her life she's ever really been able to do. It could change her whole life. And she's just one of them. It's not fair to start something like this and then drop the people flat."

"But she'll find what she needs, Betsy. Just like she found you." Max stopped. It was an old argument between them. Max would accuse her of being maternal and presumptuous—of being on an ego trip, as if without her other people wouldn't be able to cope. And she'd accuse him of being fatalistic, of being stupid about the meaning and impact of one person's actions on another. She'd call him cold.

Betsy broke the pause. "That's not what you think about Robby." Her voice was ice.

"Okay. That's not what I think about Robby," he admitted.

"But it is what you think about Sidney."

He was stung. "That's pretty shitty of you. Have you spoken to Mitzi or Lynn today?"

"Do you care?"

"Betsy, let's not do this, we'll get ourselves in a mess we can't get out of. I don't want that. I don't think you do."

"Since nothing's too much to do for Robert Rosen," Betsy shrilled.

Max felt a spurt of fury. She's jealous as well as frightened and her reaction is so childish he itched to rub her nose in it. He took a deep breath.

"Let's not do this, Betsy," he repeated, forcing himself to untense his shoulders and slowly exhaling through his mouth. There were muffled noises on the other end.

"I have some messages for you," she said thinly. "Tyrone Pendergast called."

"What? Betsy, you should have called me right away!"

"I did. I've been calling you for over an hour."

"Where was he? What did he say? Are you all right?"

"He's not here, if that's what you mean. His message is for you to butt out because he's going to get Dick Conway. He says Dick killed Shirley. I asked him why he thinks so but he wouldn't say. He just told me to tell you to stay away from Dick because you might get caught in the coils yourself. That's what he said: coils. Whatever that means. I'm pretty sure he was stoned. And he must have called from out of town because I kept him talking for a while, trying to get him to explain, and an operator interrupted. She wanted $1.85 for another three minutes. You haven't seen him, have you Max? Tell the truth!"

"No, I haven't."

"Well, I even tried to find out where the call had come from but the phone company won't tell you anything."

"The cops are checking him out. It'll be okay." Max made his voice sound much calmer than he felt.

"Actually, he apologized. Sort of. I mean he said he wouldn't have hit you the other night if you'd kept out of his way."

"I'll bear that in mind," Max said.

"I'm sure you will. Just the way you told me all about what happened between you two."

Max didn't have an answer for that one.

"Thomas Sweetwater phoned." she continued, changing back to the tone of a dutiful secretary. "He needs to speak to you." He's the Quorod gallery director and Max had spoken to him only once since his show came down.

"I'll call him tomorrow," he responded submissively.

"And Juan Carlos called."

"Oh Jesus. If he calls again, tell him I'm up in the country with no phone. *Please.*"

"Okay. And someone who said his name is Lee Sam. But he wouldn't leave a number."

"Who is he?"

"I haven't the faintest idea."

Max pinched his nose to concentrate. A friend of Sing Loo's? He didn't think so. "Chinese?"

"He telephoned, Max. I didn't see him."

"No accent?"

"I don't know," she said petulantly. "I thought he sounded sort of British. He didn't talk like Charlie Chan, if that's what you mean."

"I'm sorry. I was only trying to place him. What did he say?"

"He said hello is Max Birtwhistle there, and where were you, and when could he reach you. And I told him I'd give you his number when you called and he said there wasn't any way you could reach him and he'd have to call you back. That was it."

"Well, give him this number if he bugs you again. Okay? And I'll call you tomorrow night."

"If you want. I might be out."

"Be careful Betsy."

But she had hung up.

#

Max sat outside on Robby's front step for a while, staring out at nothing until he realized how cold he was getting. Then he went into the bedroom, wrapped himself in a sour smelling quilt, and flopped on Robby's bed. He stared at nothing some more, a mix-master operating at full tilt in his head. Now and again the face of Sharkey Pierce materialized on the cloudy ceiling, looking down at him with an annihilating glare.

He had probably slept without knowing it; the light on the ceiling was bluish grey when he realized he was still staring at the same spot. He didn't move.

Look for the wrong thing. What was the wrong thing?

Closest to hand were the men in the bar —Lenny and Sharkey and their friend Ray, the car genius. Ray must work near the bar. He'd come in wearing work clothes in mid-afternoon and he'd been wearing work clothes the other night as well. Max had seen Pierce Construction Company enough times; it was a Hargate landmark, a large white painted barn, just beyond the firehouse, easily eighty years old, with a cupola on the top. There was a newer building right beside it, a one-story affair of cinder block and corrugated steel, and behind them both a lumberyard and a lot where several trucks were usually parked. A man with a business like that can be worth a million dollars or be half a jump ahead of bankruptcy. Or both. Max squirmed uncomfortably.

Len was very likely the "Lennart Anderson Jr. - prop." per the sign on the ancient corner grocery store. Len had known Ray "all our lives." Funny only because Len looked at least ten years older than Ray. Max stared on as the ceiling grew lighter, thinking about the street, the stores, the houses. He must have dozed again. Franklin Swann was calling his name and making the front door shake with his knocks.

"Yeo!" Max called out, jolting himself with the loudness of his own voice. "Hang on, I'm coming."

Franklin was rattled. He poured out a stream of garbled apology while Max stood with cold bare feet, holding the storm door open. It took a while for Max to get what Franklin was apologizing for.

"Oh, drop it," Max finally managed to insist. "I didn't take any offence. Come on inside."

"Really, man," Franklin continued, "I mean I just hope." He was wearing a wooly sweater with big leather patches on the elbows. He was combed and washed and shiny enough for Sunday school.

"Come inside before my arm falls off. And shut up until I've had some coffee."

Franklin did as he was told. After a while, Max brought in a pot, two cups he'd washed, and a sugar bowl. He set them on top of some books and wrestled with the broken venetian blinds. "This place is a sty," he remarked as dust from the blinds swirled into the morning sun. It was another mild day, but not as beautiful as Monday. Franklin had left his MG on the shoulder of the road instead of bringing it up the eroded driveway.

"How long have you lived up here?" Max asked.

"A year and a half about," Franklin said. He wanted milk for his coffee, but Max told him there wasn't any. He revved up to apologize for asking.

"For chrissake, it's too early in the morning," Max snapped. "You asked me to sleep with you, I said no; just forget it. I'm a lot more interested in anything you know about Shirley's life up here, the people around her. You ever hang in Hargate?"

"Almost never. But I'll tell you, it's not peace and love in the countryside. It seems to me a lot of funny stuff goes on. Some of the locals are, well, hillbillies, man, really. It sort of throws you. I mean we're just sixty miles from the city."

Then he began to talk about a series of houses that had been stripped of genuine antiques while the reproductions and the cheap stuff were left behind—hardly a hillbilly caper.

"Did any of it ever turn up?"

"Helen told me they identified a grandfather clock in a shop on East 74th Street. The thing of it was, the guy had bought it from a reputable dealer in Toronto. Both of them were clean all up and down. Funny stuff, right?"

Max sipped coffee: "Shirley didn't have any valuable furniture, not up here. God knows her place didn't look like it would."

"There have been summer houses that were just plain trashed," Franklin persisted. "Tar smeared on the wall, stuff smashed up. Cops busted two, three local kids doing that last year. And a fantastic castle below Peekskill was burned down last fall after one of the high school football teams finished an unbeaten season. They never caught anyone one for that but a lot of people talked as if it was part of the celebration."

Max poured himself another cup.

"Do you pick up a lot of resentment? A lot of cold stares?"

"Almost never," Franklin admitted puzzled. "Shirley was annoyed though. Sheesh, I remember now. She had some idea about a swimming pool. She wanted to have one in the meadow alongside the house. What she really wanted was a natural pool, you know, with fieldstones.

The water in that creek comes right out of the reservoir. Should have been easy. She was really steamed. Some local guy gave her one hard time, a whole lot of bullshit about how she didn't know what she was talking about. Real nasty. So I told her fuck it, get a pool dealer in Poughkeepsie or Newburgh or something. I said I'd help her landscape it, you know, so it wouldn't look all plastic. She did it too. I was in the house with her when she called the guy and told him to stuff it. Well, I asked a few people about him after that. You know a job like that is a reasonable piece of change. It all seemed pretty weird, his being nasty. Turns out this Pierce is a bad news guy. He and two pals of his have got up a lot of folks' craws."

"Who'd you get that from?"

"I know some guys in the woodlot across the way. They save scraps for me. They both know the Pierce guy and they sure don't like him. They both said it was nothing, that it sounded just like him."

"Did they say anything else? Anything about his friends?"

"They told me Pierce has been bragging for years about how he's gonna sell out and leave. It's a popular idea, according to them, but they've given up hope that he'll really do it. One of his friends is an ace mechanic, and everybody likes him, but he's sort of under Pierce's thumb. They recommended him for my car. He's at the body shop behind the Hargate police station."

"A tall blond guy named Ray?"

"I never went. I have a friend in the city who keeps her going for me."

"Did Shirley use him?"

"She might have. I never heard her mention it. She was really steamed about the way Pierce acted though," Franklin repeated.

"It bothers me too," Max said. He drained his cup and looked absently across the room. A large ink and water color drawing he'd given Robby for a present was expensively framed on the opposite wall. Cool precise bands of color—the Max that Max liked to be—balanced, knowing, in control. It looked foolish and weak in the middle of the crazed squalor of Robby's living room. He felt himself to be more like the room than he wanted to admit. His art was thin, idealized.

"I'm leaving too much out," he said, half-aloud.

"Dick Conway?" Franklin asked.

"No. His car was in his garage all night," Max answered slowly. "Did you two know each other?"

The detective told me he and Shirley were involved. I didn't know about that."

"Did she ever mention her brother to you?"

"I didn't know she had one. We really weren't too personal, if you know what I mean."

Guess I do, Max thought; she spilled her heart out to Glazer, she slept with you, she made money with Dick, and maybe even planned to marry him, for tax purposes I wouldn't be surprised. Everything in its place and a place for everything. Was there a place for me? Or, more to the point, a place for Betsy? She wanted to depend on us for Sidney's future welfare. Betsy, practical and warm; me, professional and successful. Only she hadn't worked it out in time. It wasn't much of a priority for a healthy woman in her thirties. Damn that Irelli. I hope he took me seriously; I hope to hell he's checking the way he should.

Max began describing Tyrone and his wife for Franklin.

He'd never seen either of them, he was sure. Dick insisted Shirley was through with Tyrone. Why had Tyrone called Betsy with messages for me? Why would Tyrone say Dick had murdered Shirley?

"Dummy." Max said out loud. Shirley had changed her mind. Is that what Tyrone knows? Dick was his enemy, responsible for all her earlier hesitation about money. Whatever else Tyrone might have done, he wouldn't have beaten his sister to death but he might believe Dick had done it in a violent quarrel.

"What?" Franklin said, very red under his tan.

"Not you, man, I'm sorry. It's damn hard to put this thing together. You want to help me, Franklin?" Max asked. Franklin looked a little concerned.

"Anything you say," he volunteered in a hesitant voice.

"It's a chore, like a lot of genuine police work. Robby's got the New York phone books here. Go through the rental car listings and find out if a Richard Conway rented a car last Tuesday or Wednesday. Tell 'em, tell 'em there's a misunderstanding and he was supposed to charge it to his client's credit card, something like that, to make them check their records for you." Max hauled the yellow pages out from under the hall table. "Jesus, there are a lot of them." He held the open book out to Franklin. "It'll probably take half the morning. I want to do some poking around. If I'm not back at noon, I'll give you a call."

Franklin's relief at being given a safe task was almost comical. He was already on the phone with Avis when Max left the house.

A teenager with a sullen face pointed to a pair of feet that poked from under a crumpled Dodge. "You better wait a while," he mumbled ungraciously and ambled across the oily floor back to the car he had been buffing. The feet wore brown canvas shoes and bright green socks that disappeared up the legs of soiled white coveralls. Max watched them move, expertly positioning the dolly on which the man's body lay underneath the car. An FM station played an old Jack Teagarden piece but the sweet lines were broken by the on and off buzzing of the boy's buffer. Max leaned against the open garage door and lit a cigar.

"Hey Ace," Ray bellowed from beneath the car, "gimme the s-s-s-solvent. I'm s-s-s-stuck with this m-m-mother."

The buffer stopped. "There's a guy wants to see you," the boy answered. Ray pushed himself halfway out and looked up.

"I can wait," Max said. "I just came to shoot the breeze."

Ray shoved himself out and scrambled to his feet. He looked pale under the black smears on his face. "What can I do for you?" he asked professionally.

"I wanted to take a look at your BMW," Max was smiling.

Ray stuck his hands in the deep pockets of his coveralls. "No, you didn't," he said, dead even. There was no stutter but his lips twitched just a little.

"No, I didn't." Max smiled again. "I wanted to ask you what got into your friend last night."

The stutter came back with a rush: "Duh, duh, duh, duh," he strangled, spit flying. He shook his head violently, breathed in, and whistled breathily. The boy set a can of solvent by the empty dolly and looked with greedy curiosity at the two men.

"Don't," Ray said after a bit. "Sharkey didn't mean—" He was caught on a row of t's and the hands in the depths of his pockets were clenched so tightly cords stood out his forearms.

"He said some ugly things about my friend Shirley Pendergast. I'd like to know what he meant."

Ray nodded his head, then shook it. He pointed suddenly, foolishly, to his own head. "D-d-d-drink w-w-wa-wa-da." The stress on the last syllable was almost spastic in its intensity. Spit was dribbling from the corners of his mouth. He walked rapidly from the garage into the office, but, Max noticed, he passed the ice-water drinking fountain and passed out of sight through an interior door.

The boy looked fascinated. Max had a flood of adrenalin—he'd been looking through the glass door into the empty office.

"That door in there go to the john?"

"No," the boy said, surprised.

Max bolted through the garage door and around the front where the gas pumps were. Max looked up the alley that ran behind the garage, parallel to Main Street's row of buildings. There was the back of Ray veering sharply left and disappearing.

Max followed, fast. Ray had gone through a foot and a half wide gap between two buildings. The dirt path was brick-hard from years of use. Against the building walls, weeds competed with trash for a little light and living space. Max ran. He squinted when he cleared the corner and emerged on Main Street's sidewalk in full sunlight again. There were half a dozen people along the two sides of the street, but none was Ray. His eye caught the corner grocery store's door, swinging shut. That had to be him.

Max walked up the street. He felt as blissfully exhilarated as he did when the movement of his brush caught the tension of a piece and made the whole begin to 'work'. He took the two steps up to the raised wooden sidewalk fronting Anderson's and opened the door. The store's floor was wood, washed and walked on for a hundred years. It gleamed like grey ribbed silk. The shelves were high and crowded, separated by narrow aisles with more goods suspended above each row; a maze across which it was impossible to see. He circled a row then another, pleased despite the pressure of the chase by the mellowed juxtaposition of things: baby food and parafin, hunting gloves, school supplies, gun oil, faucet washers, dusty cans of fruit—and by the realization that Ray knows something. Max called his name. A woman by a shelf of breakfast cereal looked at him with guarded interest.

"You seen Ray?" he asked.

She shook her head and turned her face away.

A woman with badly swollen legs came slowly down the stairs at the back end of the store. From about halfway down, the outside railing was hung with blue jean jackets and brilliant rubber slickers.

"Be with you in a minute, Mrs. Deutsch," she said, taking the steps with obvious effort.

"No hurry Lil. You got any local eggs?" The woman gave Max another curious glance and carried the wire basket holding her purchases to the counter at the back end of the store where meat and dairy foods were kept in glass fronted refrigerators. She and the woman descending the stairs reached the counter at the same time.

No one else was in the store. Max turned at the front and took an empty basket from the stack by the door. There was another counter near the door and the shelves facing it showed signs that Anderson's catered to people other than long-time country residents: high-fashion sun tan oils and imported sunglasses, health food cookies piled in large glass jars. A placard suggested, "Ask about our home-baked pies" and a little freezer was stocked with frozen yoghurt and imported ice cream. Max strolled back toward the two women at the rear filling his basket with a loaf of bread, a can of tuna fish, a jar of watermelon pickles. The women's conversation lagged when he got close.

"Feel better soon," the customer urged, taking up her packages and her change.

The woman behind the counter sighed.

"I thought I'd find Len in here," Max remarked.

"I thought so too," the woman answered. Her face was puffy and marred by smudges of pain. It had been a striking face once. With delicate fingers she lifted the heavy hair from her temples half coquettishly, half as if her temples couldn't bear the pressure of it. Her chin was pointed and her dark eyebrows jutted together. "What can I do for you then?" she asked hoarsely.

"A quart of milk and a half pound of store cheese. When's he due back?"

"I don't know what to tell you, mister. Doctor says I'm not supposed to be on my feet this way. Last couple of days, I don't know what to expect. The kids are in school, I don't know what he thinks." She breathed unsteadily, pulled a long square of yellow cheese out of the icebox and set it on the slicing machine. "Sliced?"

Max nodded. She fed the cheese to the spinning knife with a rocking motion that took her whole body. Her doctor was right, her eyes were glazing and she seemed nearly out on her feet.

"That's enough," Max interrupted. "Can I get someone for you? I thought I saw his friend Ray coming in here a couple of minutes ago."

She looked up at him bitterly. "Sick as I am, my life would be A-okay if I didn't have Ray Walker and that Sharkey Pierce to worry my mind. I should of seen the light in high school. I should of read the writing on the wall."

There was a stool behind the counter. She steadied herself onto it. From her perch, she reached out for the cheese, balancing herself with the knuckles of one hand and attempting to fold waxed paper around it with the other.

"Maybe you shouldn't be here by yourself," Max said.

"Tell him!" she muttered, gesturing to the floor above.

"Len's upstairs?"

She looked flustered and then angry. "No, no, I didn't say that!" Her eyes flashed dramatically. She must have been a terror, Max thought, in a red flowered dress maybe, her skin dark from the summer sun, her large lips moist and healthy. He looked at the little landing at the top of the steps and the wooden door with a white porcelain handle.

I got my troubles, mister. So does everybody," she announced. She returned the cheese brick to its place in the dairy case and extracted a quart of milk. She punched out his purchases on the cast iron register.

"That's for sure," Max soothed. There was a thump on the floor above, and a series of rustling noises, as if furniture were being moved. They both looked up.

"Cat," she said, lying.

"Some cat," Max answered, handing her a bill.

"Don't got me wrong. Len's the sweetest guy in this county. Ask anyone. He stuck by his mother all those years and now he's, he's." Her hands were shaking. "I just don't know what's the matter with him this past week. But he's not like that. I gotta..."

"Mrs. Anderson, you oughta do what your doctor says. Close up the store, if necessary. Go back to bed."

She looked at him with dumb bewilderment; closing the store was unthinkable.

"Do it," Max said taking his paper bag. "Go upstairs and tell your husband I said so."

There were two floors over the store, a full one and an attic with dormer windows protruding from the sloping roof. Max walked into the alley, examining them. The dormers were shut, the windows on the floor below uniformly closed and shielded by drawn brown window shades. Oddly, there was no back door at all, and no outside back steps where he'd expected to find them. Max went on down the alley, toward his car. He stuck his bag of groceries in the hot back seat and locked the doors. The milk would spoil, to hell with it. Nothing could have persuaded him to leave Hargate's Main Street. He opened his jacket and undid the top buttons of his shirt. There was summer-like humidity in the warming day—and he cut quickly to the drugstore opposite the police station for the payphone.

The line at Robby's house was busy. Franklin was still tracking rent-a-cars. Max could see just the near edge of Anderson's through the plate glass by the drugstore's phone booth. The pathway to the alley was in full view and about four blocks of street. Nothing special was happening: a lone dog trotted by, a woman dragged two small girls into the shoe-repair shop. He pulled out the card Irelli had given him and dialed the number on it.

No, he was told, Detective Irelli was not available, he could leave his number and his call would be returned. No, he was not in the office, he might return late in the afternoon. Could he speak to someone else? What did this refer to? Irelli was on assignment in New York City, the man allowed reluctantly, but he would call in. Max gave his name and thanked the disembodied voice. He hung up thoughtfully. He had nothing to report at all, nothing but hunches, worries, things that didn't quite compute—things he would have see about for himself, in spite of Irelli's cautions about poking around. He got change from the druggist and rang Wilson-Hill.

Marcia answered her extension breathlessly. She was outraged at the news about Robby. "We should *do* something," she insisted. Max had to talk her out of calling up a special legal assistance program for needy artists.

"I know those people, Marcia, they help artists with tax trouble or people who want to start nonprofit groups. They don't do crime stuff. Anyway, Robby has a lawyer from Legal Aid.

"But I don't understand. Is it the money? Couldn't we raise it?"

"Robby doesn't want us to," Max said.

There was a little silence. "Pride," she said. "That breaks my heart. God."

"Well, it's *his* pride, you know. How are you?"

"Things are still pretty crazy," Marcia said more soberly. "I'm not sure what's going to happen to me. Mr. Hammer called me in this morning and said I mustn't be nervous about my job. He called me dear. It made me feel I'd better be nervous. Some of Shirley's projects are being loaded onto other editors. I don't like it. Who knows who they'll hire for Shirley's place, or how I'd fit in, or even if I will, at the rate they're going. I wish I knew what to do!"

"S'tough," Max sympathized. "Fatherly advice if you

want it: sit tight but get your resume ready. If you've got some friends somewhere else, you might just pass the word. It's always a good idea to have some options."

A lumber truck with Pierce Construction Company emblazoned on its side proceeded slowly down Main Street. A young redhead was driving it.

"I just hate feeling I'd better cut and run," Marcia sighed. "It's so—oh, Max, something strange happened this morning. I'm glad you're on the phone. Remember those papers Robby was so excited about, the one's we're holding for him? Someone called about them. He said he needs to see them. It made me feel very queer. I mean Robby wouldn't even be in trouble if he'd known the papers were here."

"Who?"

"He said his name was Sam, Mr. Sam I think, and he teaches at or is connected to some institute for Jewish history. I think he said the name but it was a little hard to understand him on the phone. Who is he? Do you know about him?"

"No." Max said slowly. "Why was he so hard to understand?"

"He talked awfully fast and he had, well he sounded German but not quite, you know? I'm usually pretty good at pegging accents. Austrian, maybe, or Swiss? Don't know why exactly, but I played dumb. Said I didn't know anything about it. Then he got pushy. Really insistent. He said he knew the papers were here, and he's on this very tight schedule, and he has to update some information he gave Robby, and I could sit in the room with him if I thought it was necessary. He went on and on. I just kept saying things were very upset because of Miss Pendergast's death and I absolutely couldn't help him. I hope I haven't insulted anyone important. I wasn't sure what to do."

"You did fine. I'll be seeing Robby today, or if not, tomorrow. I'll ask about this. Listen, if this guy calls you again, have him call me up here. Or get his number for me."

You sound serious. What is it?"

"The truth is, I don't know."

"Should I take them home? Max?"

"Why?" Max was startled.

"The vault's just a big wall safe right next to Mr. Hammer's office and three or four people around here know how to open it. People do go in and out all the time. What's Robby got in there?"

"I don't know," Max said firmly. "As far as I'm concerned, a lot of nothing and most probably this Sam character is just another of his screwball friends. But maybe you're right. It might be better if the papers weren't in the vault. It makes them look too important." He was remembering Marcia holding an accordion folder in the office hallway: "Why don't you get them back and stick them in one of the, what did you call it? the dead files? In with the old proofs of *Light Dented*. We'll know where they are but it would be damn hard for anyone else to find them. What do you think?"

Marcia giggled: "You don't know how good that is! The dead files are a total mess." Max knew from her excitement she was going to look in Robby's notebooks herself.

"Take a look yourself," he suggested, casual and off-hand. "If you've got a couple of hours. Robby's head works like a Chinese puzzle. But you were right this morning. Don't let anyone have them. I gave Robby my word."

"Got it," Marcia replied efficiently, level-headed Marcia, pleased to be a part of the plot. "We'll be in touch."

During his phone call six or seven people had collected on the round stools at the drugstore's lunch counter. The grill emitted smells of hamburger fat and bacon and the girl on duty had her hands full. The homely, slightly unpleasant smells reminded Max he needed fuel. He called Robby's house again. Franklin answered the first ring. He'd been about to leave. He had phoned every agency in Manhattan.

"Zip. None of them have anything," he complained hoarsely. "Do you think he could have used another name?"

"Pretty hard," Max answered. "Only pros have phony licenses and credit cards to match."

Franklin wanted to keep at it, checking the other boroughs and even near New Jersey. "I left you a note. There's no sense not being thorough, man. I'm going home to get some lunch. The Ockburgh's have a mess of phone books in their house, or I might go down to the phone company." He'd really gotten into it.

"Dick could have borrowed a car," Max pointed out.

"Yeah, but we can't be sure he didn't rent one unless we call every single possible place."

"True. Let me know what you find. And thanks, Franklin."

A man with coveralls just like Ray's ambled in and greeted friends at the rear counter. Max went out onto the sidewalk and stretched. He eased up the street, still keeping his eye on Anderson's. The windows had changed; a front one on the second floor was now open about five inches. The store below, though, was now dark. Max crossed over and looked in. A penciled sheet of school notepaper was taped to the inside of the glass front door. "Closed until 3:30. Please come back—Andersons," it read.

Max gave the building another once-over. The alley was on one side and on the other side it shared a wall with the next building over, a flat roofed building only two storys high. It would be easy to get out of the Anderson's dormers and onto its roof. From there one could make way across the uneven row of roofs facing Main Street and it would be hard to see anything from the street. Almost all the buildings had projecting fronts, vanity facades to make their fronts more impressive. Max realized now the next-door building served as storage for the store. The windows were blocked by bars and boxes and it was undoubtedly connected by interior doors. Ray had probably left quietly by the door that opened on the alleyway Max had used, and returned to Main via that footpath.

At the drugstore, he checked the Newburgh directory for an Esther Williams swimming pool company. The woman who answered his call was very apologetic. Their preliminary surveying had been delayed by rain but they had it re-scheduled for this coming Saturday and there was no reason why work wouldn't begin on April 15th, exactly as they'd promised. Max had to tell her there was a reason why. He gave her Starkazi's number so they could make arrangements to return Shirley's deposit to her estate.

The call had smothered his appetite. He sat down on the last stool at the rear counter, trying to decide whether to go back to the garage or drive over to Maquaset and visit Robby. The peripatetic Mr. Sam was beginning to annoy him like cracker crumbs in bed.

The counter girl apparently recognized him. She batted eyes clumsy with fake lashes and Max tried to keep his own eyes fixed on the menu board above her head while he ordered. She tried the eye business again when she brought his sandwich and smiled a bit nervously as she explained the rolls "were real fresh."

He thanked her gravely and watched her perform for him as she went back down the counter to other customers, wagging her hips. Something in her manner suggested she had a claim on him. Max wasn't amused.

"Hey fella," the counter girl said, returning with a damp rag for cleaning the counter.

"Yeah?"

"I heard some people talking." She examined a chip on one of her polished fingernails. Then she tossed her head back. In TV commercials, a wind machine lifts the hair when models do that; hers simply flopped against her cheek.

"What's that?" Max used a tone of patient forbearance.

"Your name's Birdzipper?" She cocked her head.

"Birtwhistle, Max Birtwhistle. I think that guy down there needs something." Max made a gesture and stuffed a large bite of sandwich in his mouth. He turned on his stool and looked out toward the street, chewing methodically, but the counter was too far back from the window for him to see much.

"Far out," the girl said. She was back, this time with a fresh paper cup of water which she exchanged for his half empty one. "You a writer too, like your friend?"

"No. And I don't need the water as much as another cup of coffee, thank you."

"You bet. Pie? The coconut custard's not so bad. I wouldn't recommend the apple though." She curled her lips to indicate distaste and licked at the corners where the lipstick had caked.

"Just the coffee."

She returned with it. She pushed the cream pitcher closer to his arm. Max was beginning to feel claustrophobic. All but one of the other customers had finished and the lunchtime rush, if you could call it that, was over. Max tried washing his sandwich down with gulps of coffee. She leaned against the sandwich board opposite in a posture that pushed up her padded bra.

"Birtwhistle, wow. What kind of name's that?"

"Mine," said Max.

She laughed over hard. Max asked for his check.

"Wait a minute, wait a minute, please." She looked nervously across the store at the man in front. From his white coat, he was obviously the druggist and just as obviously her boss. "I gotta talk to you. I mean it. Listen," she continued rapidly in a lowered tone of voice. Max stood up and reached for his wallet.

"Please!"

Max nodded a little. "I've got things to do," he said.

"Me too. I don't know how to say this but could we talk later, you know, after I get off? I. . ." she trailed off. She was embarrassed now. The stylized movements left her and she clutched at the edge of the lunch counter, an anxious, guilty child behind a painted adult face. "I gotta tell you something. I mean it."

Max looked at her carefully. "When do you get off?"

"Not here man. J'yuh know the custard stand, north on 9? I'll be there at five o'clock. I like you," she said, again scanning the drugstore.

"I'll buy you an ice cream but I won't be able to stay long."

She shot him an insulted look. "I've said I've got something to tell you," she hissed. "I'm nobody's fool."

"Keep it that way."

Conspiracy was written on her like a billboard as she took his money and returned in a moment with his change. "Five o'clock, don't pull a number on me now."

"You either." Max returned, but she was cool now, back under control. She briskly scooped up his soiled dishes and dumped them in the dishpan underneath the soda fountain.

In spite of himself Max began to feel horny, and angry about it. She'd be about as much fun as a Disneyland mannequin, he scolded himself. If you were gonna get after the teenage stuff think of all the students you've by-passed, lovely girls, quick and bright and full of themselves, easy and adventurous . . . Max, stop it! You're making it worse.

He stopped. He was on the sidewalk in front of a glass-fronted office. Real Estate - Insurance. Established 1923. "Country property" a neatly lettered sign suggested. Max opened the front door and stepped onto a dark red rug. A man behind a wooden desk looked up and smiled.

"Do something for you?"

"Maybe. I want to ask some questions, anyway." They exchanged names and shook hands briefly. Max was offered a leather bottomed chair.

"I'm thinking about a country place, something my wife and I would use mainly in the summer. But if we buy, I want something okay for winter weekends too. We need a fair amount of space for working. I paint and my wife's a potter. A small house would be fine if it's got useable outbuildings, a chicken house, stable, small barn—something we could convert to studio space. But we can't afford to get into anything that needs really major reconstruction."

"Ever think of commuting?" the man asked. He was somewhere around fifty, settled and comfortable with himself, putting on middle weight with his middle years. He wore glasses with half clear rims that mildly magnified his pale blue eyes; a white handkerchief protruded nattily from the breast pocket of his dark brown jacket.

"I don't think I could hassle that."

"Not as bad as you might think," the agent suggested. "A number of people who began as summer residents are living all year round up here. They drive on down to Peekskill and pick up the fast train."

Max looked cautious.

"I've heard talk from people about trouble with empty houses in the winter. It's not a good idea to leave a place empty, is that right?"

"Not at all, not at all," the agent doubled back quickly, it was only that the area is wonderful all year round and he, personally, is delighted to see artistic people moving in. "Good for the community," he gushed. "Couldn't be better. To be frank, you might have heard that a boy with mental problems caused some trouble last year. He was caught right away. He's now in a special school."

The agent pointed at the county map on the office wall bedabbled with large irregular areas of green and brown. "This part of the county is a natural for artistic people," he continued. "Nearly half the land is state forest, state park, or watershed preserve. It's rural and the wooded character will always be preserved."

Max asked about developers. The agent had a little trouble with his answers. He wanted to boast about progress, new schools, expanded shopping, centers for this and that—but he knew what kind of customer he was dealing with. Max would be the sort who'd get uneasy about malls and suburb communities, no matter how beautifully planned.

Max pressed him saying he was particularly interested about any possible development in the Horse Creek Road vicinity.

The agent laughed gesturing at the map again. A developer would be out of his mind over there—the private land along Horse Creek Road was too limited to be of use. Only narrow lots. In some places the state land reached right to the roadbed.

"But, if you're interested in a building without much property," he said thoughtfully "there is a barn up there that was fixed up as an artist's studio back in the forties. I think the fellow was a cartoonist, a friend of Mrs. Hendrix's son. It's been empty for years and years. Don't know what kind of shape it's in, but if you're interested,

I'll make an inquiry. Old Mrs. Hendrix, she's a little strange since her husband died." He shook his head. "It's a shame. Hendrix was quite a family, quite a family around here. Good Lord, she's got to be over eighty by now," he mused. His eyes roamed the little office as if he expected to see her there. "Her children aren't coming back here, that's for sure."

His eyes refocused on Max and the present tense. "It just might be worth us asking if she'd think about it," he said, pursing his lips shrewdly and watching Max's face for agreement.

"I'd have to look at it first," Max said. The agent was taken back: if a Hendrix were willing to part with Hendrix property, one should feel honored, almost awed. He leaned back in his chair to explain.

"Hundreds of acres of what's now state forest used to be Hendrix farms. For generations. They *were* the local society. Old Mr. Hendrix, of course, hadn't been a farmer himself; no, no, he was a naturalist, a fellow at Columbia University, a pillar of the National Geographic Society, a donor, mind you, to the New York Museum of Natural History. Very established people, the Hendrixes, and old Mr. Hendrix wanted to see the county's natural resources protected for future generations."

Nostalgia ran thick in the little room. He went on: The Hendrix daughter had been in grammar school with him, that was before she left for boarding school, then Europe for her music studies. Each time she visited her old home she was more exotic and wonderful—but life isn't always what you expect; she'd broken her father's heart. There were marriages, love affairs, and after her only child died, she never came home. She must be living somewhere in Europe. . . .

"I've been up Horse Creek Road once," Max interrupted the river of reminisce. "A friend took me up there to visit his editor. She was killed there last week. I'm sure you know about it. That's one of the reasons I asked about vandals."

The agent snapped out of the past; his spine stiffened and he looked intently at Max through his glasses. "Bad business," he said grimly. "Bad business. I don't like to say anything about the lady, you understand, so I hope I'm not offending you—but the local police seem to think it may have been a lovers' quarrel that got out of hand. I hope they clear it up soon. Terrible business."

"Yes, yes it is. I'm curious, though, did Mrs. Hendrix sell that property to Miss Pendergast?"

"Good lord, no! That little section was a thorn in the Hendrix side for a hundred years. There was nearly a feud between them and the Andersons about it. No matter what the Hendrix family did, the Andersons wouldn't part with it. My dad told me, as a matter of fact, old Mr. Hendrix offered them three thousand dollars for it. That would have been just before World War I when three thousand dollars was a sizeable sum of money. Nope. What's more I think Howard Anderson built that shack just for spite. He was quite the character. If you saw it you know. It was made up of bits and pieces of torn down buildings from all over. He used to go up there when he was angry at his wife. The odd part is, I was always afraid he'd burn himself up out there. He'd be sitting out on that high porch, drinking all night, and smoking big cigars.

We couldn't believe it when we heard he actually sold it. He'd sworn he'd never part with it. And his nephew tried to have him declared incompetent to void the sale. But don't you know, the old man died. Just keeled over one day, not more than three months later. Personally I think the old bastard—pardon me— I think he knew he was about to go and sold it to the Pendergast lady just to annoy everybody."

"Are Andersons and Hendrixes still mad at each other?"

"I suppose it's all over now. Anderson's widow got a little money from the sale, not much, but I don't think she cared one straw about the place. And Mrs. Hendrix said as long as it was out of Anderson hands she wasn't going to let it bother her any longer. I believe Len was bitter though. He's the nephew. You know how things like that can be in a family. He claimed his uncle had always promised to leave that place to him, but, well, I'm sure it's all forgotten now. There was no point to it anyway. The lot is a queer triangle, not good for much. And that shack! It was nothing to quarrel over.

"Way back sometime," the agent went on, "one of the Anderson's kept his pigs there. That's what started it, I believe. The Anderson family is just as stiff-necked and stubborn as anything on earth. To tell the truth, I wish that property could be given to the Girl Scout camp and be done with it. It's caused more trouble around here than it was ever worth. It's..." he groped for a word; "*ironic*." he said. "Now I've got some nice listings I think you might be interested in. Let me show you some pictures."

It was after two. Max took fifteen minutes politely

examining fuzzy photographs and padded descriptions of abandoned farmhouses. The pictures made him sad. Where had the people gone? What did they have now, after their years of beating the ground to make it yield? His dad's father had spent his last days in a county home near Johnson City, Tennessee. Mercifully, he was too daffy to realize he was living on county charity. It would have killed him to know that.

He thanked the agent for his time and promised to come back with his wife. "I don't want to look at anything without her. You know how it is," he finished up.

Chasing Ray

He was behind time; he'd have to push if he wanted to see Robby and make it back for his five o'clock rendezvous with the drugstore girl. He drove impatiently using the whole paved space on the nearly empty road the way race drivers do—and to hell with the risk that a car might appear on a blind curve in the opposite lane.

Some of the best work an artist does is wasting time. Was that in an essay he'd read? Max slowed down a little. No, someone had said it at a party, someone ridiculous, affected, someone who had no idea how that statement might resonate. It has just enough truth in it to irritate. No, Max decided, it's not so irritating; it explains a lot about the living I've done. He was remembering, Juan Carlos had said it, of course, damn his agile mind and his dilettante soul.

The story he'd heard in the real estate office rolled gently in his mind—it felt like a slender core, like one of those drillings geologists make to figure out the history of a mountain or an ocean floor. He was thinking it through when he caught up with a car, halted at a crossroad stop sign. Max peered idly through its back windshield and met Ray Walker's eyes reflected in the rear view mirror. Max honked, two blips, stuck out his hand, waved.

The car ahead lept across the intersection. Max followed.

"Hey, wait a minute. Hold on!" he shouted, manipulating the Volvo to keep up. He honked again. Ray swerved onto a side road. It was a dirt road overlaid with rough gravel and both cars were now doing nearly sixty. The Volvo was almost out of control. The back end couldn't grip; the tires sprayed loose rocks and the springs jarred violently.

Ray's car had two exhausts and his muffler needed some work because his motor roared angrily. Max began to fall behind. A cloud of road dust marked Ray's passage. Max let up a little, settled the car, and let the gap between them remain steady. Following, he turned once, then again. The gap was now too big to be comfortable.

He accelerated down a steep hill with treacherous ruts along the shoulders, took a curve, and caught up in time to see Ray's car turn onto a narrow paved road that would leave no dust trail.

"You're not gonna get away from me," Max hollered. He bent to the work of making good on his pledge and felt a surge of reminiscent pleasure: high school fantasies of mastery and endurance. Hey, he could have had a case of moonshine in his trunk or been doing Le Mans for twenty-four hours.

There was dust in his mouth and sweat trickling between his shoulder blades. Ray turned again. By this time, Max was very close. He took the curve feeling body and mind fuse, the ecstasy of concentration he'd first tasted in the beautiful Birtmobile, and sometimes but very rarely lately, when deep in work on a painting. The Volvo's speedometer swung up past eighty. Awareness of his pleasure swelled like a bubble. "Stirling Moss!" he sang out, remembering the name of his favorite race driver.

The break in concentration cost him. Ray's car

vanished over a hill crest. When Max gained it, the road beyond was bare. He downshifted, cursing himself.

Three mailboxes stood at the edge of a dirt road to the left. But nothing stirred on it. The weeds at the road edge were still and the slightly sandy surface was undisturbed. A few hundred yards further, a paved driveway cut through a stand of pines. Max turned onto it. The driveway circled up hill to a pink and grey mobile home, onto which an extension that doubled its size had been attached. Ray's car was there, empty, and parked where the drive widened to provide playing space for a basketball hoop fastened to the pink windowless back wall of the extension.

Max parked. A path of the same material as the driveway led to the front door. There, wide cinderblock steps had been installed. Cinderblocks filled in the space between the ground and the bottom of the trailer too. Painted grey to match. Half a dozen infant bushes were planted in a row in front. On the edges of the steps stood two ornate plaster urns holding the dead stalks of last summer's geraniums.

Max got out and walked up to the entrance. A yellow plastic dump truck without wheels lay on the path. There were signs of childish digging in the dried thatch by the edge of the paving. From inside, a TV game show blared indistinctly.

One of the front window curtains twitched a little and the volume of the TV went down abruptly. Max could hear a woman's voice protesting and questioning. He went up the steps and rapped at the glass storm door.

The woman's voice was shrill. "What's wrong? Who is he?"

The answer, if there was one, was inaudible.

Max rapped again.

There was running inside, and some children's voices. "In the bedroom, Mikey," the woman's voice ordered fiercely.

"Mrs. Walker, let me talk to Ray a minute," Max called. He tattooed the glass firmly.

Still no sound from Ray, only the woman's voice in a frantic mumbling torrent. Then silence.

"Mrs. Walker!"

"If you don't go I'll call the cops!" She was just on the other side of the door, screaming. Then, only a little less loud: "Oh, Debby, don't!" Then noise of hands clapping as she boomed out "Deborah! Michael!" which was followed by shouts and wails, and a small girl keening, "Daddy, I'm scared."

"There's nothing to be scared of. I just need to talk to your Daddy." Max announced loudly. He felt like a first-class skunk.

"Leggo my arm, I don't care what you say, I'm calling them." Her voice was piercing.

"You're hurting my mommy," an older child shrieked. Something fell over with a clatter.

"Please, mister, please go away." She was by the door again, her voice thick with tears. "My husband's very sick."

Max walked back down the steps. He turned the car around carefully and drove slowly down the driveway, as he reached the bottom he realized he had no idea where he was. Screaming voices from the house above seemed to follow him.

He was hopelessly muddled. After twenty-five minutes of trying to backtrack, he stopped at a solitary store by the intersection of two unmarked graveled roads. A 1930's vintage gasoline pump stood in the dusty ground in front of the porch.

"Where is this?" Max asked a plump woman who came to the door.

"Wilson's Corners." She grinned toothily.

"This is it?" The two roads ran past through unused woodland.

"This is it. You lost?"

"Sure am. I need a phone." That was fine by her.

Max called Legal Aid in Maquaset and spoke a little with the young attorney who had been appointed to Robby's case. Yes, he admitted, Max would be able to see Mr. Rosen this afternoon, but what purpose would it serve? It was obvious he'd like to wash his hands of the whole business. Max groped for a way to appeal to him. The name of the publishing house made a dent. It surprised the lawyer that the nutcase he was dealing with was actually a legitimate published writer. Max could almost hear him shift gears. Of course he'd inquire if Robby had authorized a Mr. Lee Sam to examine his special files—and finally he even gave Max his home phone number so Max could call him back in the evening.

Then Max dialed the state police. Irelli had not returned. Max was relieved. The store phone booth—the only modern equipment in the place—was an unbelievably stark stand with no privacy, only three abbreviated acoustical tile wings. The plump woman had parked herself on a cane-bottomed stool and was listening so hard her mouth had dropped open. Max asked the cops for a call-back at Robby's number after seven.

"It's important. I need to be sure he's received my message." He repeated his name and the phone number, slowly and distinctly. The cop on the other end was patiently annoyed.

"Highway 9's just over that way," the plump woman gestured vaguely when Max was through with the phone. One of her front teeth was badly chipped and it caught on her lower lip. She mumbled directions citing landmarks by their local names: ". . .then turn left at Robert's farm, go on up to the fork at Cooper's and you cain't miss it!" she finished up.

Max hadn't the foggiest idea how to use her instructions. He thanked her and got out fast.

AT THE DAIRY QUEEN

It was quarter past five by the time he pulled into the Dairy Queen on Highway 9. It was the only open enterprise in a clump of derelict amusements: a weed-grown miniature golf course, an abandoned drive-in movie, a brick building boasting pool and beer that had strips of boarding nailed across its broken windows.

The girl from the drugstore was in the parking lot at the wheel of a red Camaro. She glared at him. He got out and walked over to her open window.

"I was just about to split, you know."

"You want something?" he asked. She did. He slid into the passenger side of her car a few moments later handing her a double-thick strawberry shake. He had a coke for himself which was three-quarters shaven ice. She fiddled with the radio dial bringing up a hard rock station. "Some car, huh?" She gestured at the black plastic leatherette seats and the white fake fur that covered the inside walls and dashboard.

"Is it yours?" Max strained over the din. She said something, shaking her head.

"Can we turn this *down?*"

"My brother's," she repeated, and lowered the volume.

"Well?" he asked.

"You wanna go some place?"

"Not especially." He squinted at the evening sky through the tinted windshield. "I turn into a pumpkin in about a half an hour."

She leaned over the steering wheel giggling. "Far out," she wheezed.

222

"I don't know your name."

She shrugged.

"Oh, come on."

"Fran."

"Fran? That's it?"

She looked uncomfortable.

"Well, then, Fran, what's this all about?"

"It's Francesca, really." She was trying that thing with her eyelashes again.

Max felt sickened by his foolish stubbornness. Been a real asset to the community today, he was thinking—terrifying little children and now encouraging a teenage temptress. He set his coke on the dashboard and pulled at the door handle. "Okay, honey, I'll see you around," he said as pleasantly as he could.

"Wait, wait a minute. I heard something." Max had one foot on the ground.

"What about?"

"You know."

"No." He pulled his other leg out of the car as she grabbed for his arm; the seat was low and the angle was in her favor.

"About the fire. They're gonna fix it so your friend gets busted for it," she said rapidly.

Max got back in the car. "Who is they?"

"Some people."

"Francesca, a woman was murdered. Who is they?"

"I just wanted you to know. They're gonna hide something in his house."

"*Who?*"

"I think it's a hammer," she faltered. She was frightened by his expression.

"His house has already been searched," he said sternly, keeping his eyes on her face.

"They said they was gonna put it under his front steps," she whispered.

"Who told you? Someone told you?"

"No, no, I heard 'em, s'truth. I wouldn't lie to you."

"When was this?"

"Please, I could get in a lotta trouble. Yesterday? I think you're awful cute," she said wistfully. "I think you must be a real beatnik."

The impulse to shake her made his arms tingle. It was as if there were a layer of jelly between her and the real world.

He put his hand on her shoulder paternally. "Listen, Francesca, do they know you heard them?"

"No, no. I was in the back."

"You sure they didn't see you?"

"They was inside. They didn't know I was out there.

"Did *anyone* see you?"

"Noooo," she said as if he were simple minded. "It was two in the morning. There wasn't anyone there."

"And the men were inside?" She nodded again. "Why were you there?"

"That's it," she said, that was all she planned to say. "You should watch it."

"And this was last night?"

She nodded cautiously.

"Why should I believe you Francesca?"

She drew in her breath sharply and under the lipstick her narrow lips clamped. She tossed her hair and turned the car on. Max grabbed her hand and forced it to turn the key off. "Look, lady, I don't know you and I don't know your friends." She was struggling energetically to get out from under his restraining hands. "For all I know, someone sent you to set me up. Is that it?" He had both her arms pinned. The steering wheel dug into his side. She went limp suddenly—a 1940's movie dissolve into romantic soft-focus. She parted her lips, panting a little; her eyes half closed. Her face was only a few inches from his.

Max let go and sat back in the seat on his side. She looked for an instant terribly disappointed but recovered herself by smoothing out her skin-tight tee shirt and adjusting the creases of her white jeans. "These pants cost me twenty-seven bucks." She stroked the cloth on her thighs proudly.

"You better tell me all of it," Max said kindly.

"I'm scared." Maybe she was.

"Me too," Max agreed. "Me too."

She was doing a little girl number now, looking from one of his eyes to the other to demonstrate trusting vulnerability. She gestured at the pack of cigarettes on the furry dashboard and Max shook one out for her and lit it with the lighter that had been lying by the pack.

"I was waiting for someone behind Valley Auto," she said slowly. "Last night. You know." She blew out a cloud of smoke. This was her moment.

"That the place behind Len's grocery?"

"Yeah. And the person didn't show, you know? So I heard these people talking and I thought maybe it was him, right?"

Max nodded encouragingly.

"I went up to the wall so's I could hear them inside. They were all like yelling. They were really hot and Mr.

Pierce said—." She stopped, horrified.

"Yeah, Sharkey Pierce," Max soothed. "What did he say?"

"Please, I shouldn't of said that."

"It's okay, Francesca. What did he say?"

Well, he was screaming about settling something once and for all, 'cause they'd been screwing up for like fifteen years. That's what he said. And then they began talking about your friend, how he's in jail, and everybody knows he, well, you know, I mean they said everybody knows he killed his girl friend and all the cops need is just one thing to prove it. Then, um, Mr. Pierce said if they didn't do what he said about the hammer, they were just hopeless assholes." She looked uneasily past him as she spoke and picked at the padded cover of the steering wheel with a fingernail.

"Why?" Max asked.

"I don't know. I was scared they'd hear me."

"You were outside?"

"Yeah, right on the other side of the wall. I mean it, I was scared shitless. I could hear one of them laughing like he was completely nuts and Mr. Pierce went on and on about what a bad scene your friend was and how they were like doing a service getting rid of him. So I split. I don't even know if Jeff ever came. I haven't seen the bum all day, and if he thinks I'm gonna call him, he can think again."

She flipped her half-smoked cigarette out of the window.

"Who were the other men? No games, Francesca."

"I didn't really see anybody."

"You heard them. Who?"

"Ray Walker and Mr. Anderson," she mumbled, "but Ray didn't say much."

"You want to do something for me, honey?" The endearment came through loud and clear. She looked up, lips parted. Max backed away just a little and put his hand over her wrist. "Come over to Maquaset with me and make a statement to my friend at the S.B.I."

She yanked her hand away and stiffened. "What do you think I am?"

"There's nothing to be afraid of. I'll stay with you the whole time. Believe me, it'll be totally confidential."

"In the first place, I don't have anything to do with cops," she asserted. "And even if I did, how do you think I could do a thing like that? If my dad ever found out I was out of the house like that he'd kill me."

"You and Jeff have a thing?"

"Me and Jeff do not have a thing. And it's none of your damn business. Forget it. Just forget the whole thing, man. Cops! I can picture that. I sure didn't expect that from someone like you! Damn! I gotta go." She tried to lean across him to open up his door. Max opened it himself.

"And listen," she said as he climbed out, "Don't get any big ideas. If you tell anyone what I said, I'll say you're a liar. I'll tell 'em how you tried to rape me. You le' me alone!"

"Easy does it, Fran, it's a bad business," Max said, echoing the real estate agent's phrase. He shut the car door. She flashed him a furious look, turned the radio up full blast, and backed away. Her tires left two black smears on the pale concrete as she slammed the Camaro onto the highway.

Cold wind was blowing grey clouds across a black sky. Hargate Corners had rolled up its sidewalks for the night. The day that had been mild enough for open shirts rattled away in wind and dampness that could well be a hard frost by morning.

Anderson's store was locked tight. It was impossible to tell if there was any life on its upper floors; with windows shut and blinds down the building could have been ten years abandoned. Max stopped at the street's single pedestrian traffic light and watched it tell nonexistent people, "Walk."

The real estate agent's patched neon sign gleamed on the empty sidewalk. The drugstore was still open though. Max drove past, to the end of the little town. Pierce Construction Company was lit by a high spotlight in the truck lot that shone down on damp truck bodies and by another spot that illuminated the name painted on the old barn's cupola. The gates of the truck lot were fastened with a chain and padlock.

Max turned around and circled back. He drove up Main again, looking at the row of fronts and the names on some of them and the dates. Why? Why Anderson and Walker? Pierce was a miserably familiar bully and bigot but what could Shirley Pendergast have meant to any of them? A land feud that went back to their grandfathers'time? And for what? A steep hillside with a creek; a triangular lot hardly two acres? Now with a burned-out ruin and a bad story. It would probably go up for sale sometime later, maybe next fall, when Shirley's affairs were settled, or it could stay in limbo for years. It would never revert to the Andersons. Would Lennart Anderson have killed a human being to get possession of it? Len with a sick wife, with children to look after, with a business that must be hurting as highways and shopping centers made their way up from Westchester. It was all wrong.

Max parked in front of the drugstore and went in. He wanted to have someone with him when he pried the boards off Robby's little stoop. If anything had been hidden there, he wanted a witness and he wanted someone to talk to too. The grill at the back of the store was dark and the druggist was behind the prescription counter using his typewriter.

"Closing in about five minutes," he warned, not really looking up.

Franklin answered Max's call with his mouth full. Sure he'd come right over. He had some beer too and he'd bring it; he'd called forty-three car rental places, he bragged. What a day! Not one of them had Richard Conway on their records.

"Can we be sure, Max? The more I check, the more paranoid I get."

"Well, we can be sure about forty-three of them anyway. I've got some other stuff going on. Tell you when I see you. I'll be waiting here."

Max went out and sat in his car. After a while he turned the motor on and got the heater going. Someone tapped on the glass. Len Anderson was leaning down; he had a heavy plaid hunter's jacket on. His hands were jammed down in the pockets and the collar was turned up. Max rolled his window down. Wind blew the man's words away.

"...needs talk to you," he repeated.

"What's on your mind?"

"Not here, Birtwhistle. Come up to my place."

This'll have to do," Max insisted.

"It's Ray, Ray Walker. . . he's real upset."

"I'm not surprised."

"What's that?" Len shouted.

Max cut the motor of the car and put his head out the window into the gushing wind. "I'm sure he is upset. I think he's got good reason."

"Listen, he's up at the store. He wants to talk to you."

"He could have talked to me this afternoon."

"He told me that. I'm telling you—he wants to explain. Give a little, will you? It's just over there."

"Go get him, I'll wait for you." Max didn't move.

"Look, he won't come out, I'm telling you. Truth is, he's been crying. Will ya come in and talk to him. For God's sake, man." Len's face was in shadow but his voice shook emotionally. Max snapped on the Volvo's interior light. Len's eyes were bloodshot and watery. Don't go, Max's stomach told him.

"There's a lot about Ray you don't understand," Len said. "I've known the guy my whole life. Give him a minute, huh? It might clear up a lot of things."

"No way," Max said. "He can dry his eyes and come on out here if he wants. He can get in my car."

Len's face seemed to bend in for a second; then it bulged out. His eyes popped, his lips advanced, the pouches and jowls of his haggard face swelled with fury.

"I've had all I can take from you bastard," he screamed. "I'm *sick* a your shit. I'm sick a' their shit. My whole fuckin life I've done nothing but take it—do this Len, do that Len, I'm sick, Len, I'm broke, Len, I'm scared, Len, but oh no, we can't do what *you* say, Len." Spittle was flying from his mouth: "Get the fuck out of the car, man."

The gun in his hand was aimed at Max's nose. He raised his other hand to it and clicked off the safety catch. "Now!" he said. The word came from his belly, deep and vibrant. Max did what he said.

As he got out, he glanced desperately at the lighted drugstore window—the druggist must still be there, but where? behind the tallest counter? Len backed up a few steps keeping his weapon level.

"Up the street." he said.

From a great distance, Max knew his legs were doing what they were told, very, very slowly. The barrel of the gun was pressed firmly against his back just above his left hip. His brain raced like something in a mad scientist's laboratory, babbling and flashing, processing utter trivia. He'd forgotten to enter a check on the stub in his bankbook; there was a parking ticket behind the bathroom mirror, he couldn't remember whose; Betsy was embarrassed because he'd never thanked her mother for the flowers she sent when his show opened.

Stop that and think! a voice in his head demanded.

They had stopped at the door of the building next to the store. Len reached around him and opened it. The gun barrel jabbed against his hip again and the noises inside his head switched off.

They proceeded down a narrow aisle between high stacks of boxed goods. The room had the dry, closed smell of undisturbed dust; it was dark in front but shadows from a light at the other end made an overlapping pattern of grays, blacks, and dirty ochre on the ceiling. Max heard Sharkey's voice before he saw him.

"Suffering Jesus, Walker. You sound like an old woman. We got a chance to fix the whole damn thing. Just like I said last night."

Max stepped into the open area at the back where a light bulb hung over a rust-stained sink. Ray Walker was sitting on a barrel of sweeping compound hunched over with his arms wrapped tight against his belly. That much was true—he had been crying. Sharkey paced in front of him, gesturing with a large unlit cigar. He whirled around when Max approached, taking in Len and the gun with instant approval.

"It's about time you got some sense, Len. Now we're cookin."

"W- w- what's that sup- p- posed t t mean?" Ray demanded, stepping off the barrel.

"What d'yuh think it means," Sharkey's face made a quick smile at Max. "We waste the creep."

"A- z- z- zat all you can think of?" Ray shrieked. "More killing t- t- t- time, and do it again? M- m- mess we're in!" he managed.

His face was purpling. He waved a long forefinger in Sharkey's face: "N- no one was gonna be there, you said, empty, b- b- b- b- she, she."

"She was." Len finished for him.

"Keep out," Ray snarled at him. "I never know what what what side you g' g' play."

"You keep your hand outta my face!" Sharkey grabbed at Ray's arm and shoved it back. "Just cause you can't talk normal. He's in our way so we waste him. What the hell else? Sit around and let him turn us in? Then we do what we should a done years ago. Get that fucking money and split this town! Wasting my time with these jackass games." He turned his head and spat on the floor. "Hanging out with you two losers, whining and mewing year after year...."

He was so wound up he didn't see it coming. Ray punched him hard in the diaphragm just below his ribs.

Sharkey staggered up from the box he'd landed against, struggling for breath and grabbing at his jacket pocket. Wheezing, he produced a small pearl-handled pistol. Ray dove for the arm that held it. Still wheezing, the big man kicked at Ray's legs and they both fell grappling against a pile of dusty aluminum kettles—the oversized ones used for home preserving.

"Stay right where you are," Len ordered Max; he jiggled his gun for punctuation. Pots clanged and flew across the floor; the two men scuffled frantically; Sharkey's gun went off. Len didn't move. The shot had gone wild. Cartons toppled with the muffled sound of breaking inside. The pressure of Len's gun against Max's side remained unchanged.

Still holding Sharkey's arm, Ray grappled until his fingers found a kettle lid; it dented harmlessly against Sharkey's head. Suddenly he lost his grip on the arm holding the pistol. The two men separated, scrambled half way up, and crouched facing each other.

"We're gonna do this right this time," Sharkey panted

aiming at Ray. Ray shook his head. "You miserable c- c-cocksucker."

Sharkey squeezed the trigger. "I'll see you dead before I let you screw me up again," he finished when the sharp noise subsided. He was so full of venom the words were slow, flat, and without inflection. The smoky tang of gunpowder permeated the room.

Ray had been thrown up against the wall underneath the sink. Liquid seeped under his shoe and flowed in a little stream over the floor toward Max's feet. Urine, Max realized.

"Dear god!" Len said.

"You with me?" Sharkey asked him. The pistol was pointed at Len. Len released the pressure on Max and walked toward Ray like a sleepwalker. He knelt; his gun was hanging in his fingers forgotten. He put it on the floor and pulled Ray gently free of the wall sliding him out until he lay full length. Ray's legs shook, flexed up spasmodically, then flopped limp. There was a pit in the middle of his chest filling with dark red blood. His face was smooth, without expression. Len made a retching kind of groan.

"Well?" Sharkey demanded.

"He's dead. He's dead, Sharkey."

"You in or out? It's all the same to me."

"Ray's dead, you crazy son of a bitch."

"Don't you call me crazy. I'm crazy for listening to you two all these years. Two hundred thousand dollars and we ain't supposed to touch it. Listening to a stuttering creep and a hen-pecked storekeeper. You're fuckin-A that's crazy. I shoulda made a move years ago. Put him in the truck." He waved his pistol at the still figure on the floor. "And him too," he waved at Max. "Drive up to the place and get that bread up. Fifteen fucking years in the ground. You ready or not?"

Len tensed into a crouch. He's picked up his gun again and both hands were on it as he aimed at Sharkey.

Sharkey fired.

Max hit the floor covering his head with both arms. He heard Len fire back three rapid shots and the crashing noise of Sharkey toppling. When he looked up Len was rising, unevenly, from the floor; blood was running down his left arm from a tear at the top of his shoulder. Standing up, he shot into Sharkey again. Max got up. Len shot into Sharkey again. Then he looked over at Max with a sad, exhausted smile and tried to put his mouth around the smoking barrel but his lips recoiled reflexively from the heated metal.

Max leapt for him. "No," he said. "Stop." He took Len's arm, lifted his fingers out of the gun grip—they were as lifeless as old rubber, and pushed the safety on. Len sagged to the floor and laid his head against Ray's legs.

"Me and my bright ideas," he said.

RED

Max opened the connecting door and went into the darkened store. The door at the top of the steps in back was open a little and in the half-light Max could make out a boy, about eleven years old crouched on the landing with his hands gripping the railing.

"Where's your mother?" Max yelled up at him.

The boy stared, frozen.

"Your dad's okay but someone's been hurt. Tell your mother."

"She's with Aunt Rosemary." He began down the steps toward Max.

"Don't come down here!" Max commanded. The boy stopped a split-second, then turned and darted back up through the door at the top of the stairs. "Tell your aunt to come over right away and get you!" Max shouted after him. "Can you call her?"

He got to the store's main light switches and found the telephone by the front counter; he told the state police to bring Irelli with them, then went back into the storeroom. Len was lying where he'd left him with his head on Ray's legs. Max tried not to look at Sharkey.

"What money?" Max asked.

"Ours." Len didn't look up. "Sharkey really did most everything. And me. All Ray did was drive the car." He jerked his chin sideways toward the shattered shape on the floor. "We were the bright boys, we were the untouchables."

Max sat on the floor near Len and looked at him.

"Ever heard of it?" Len whispered.

"It was a TV program," Max said. "The Untouchables."

"We wore masks. Just like Brinks. Mine was Nitti. Sharkey had Ness. And baseball caps and white workman's gloves. We used toy guns! Even left 'em at the scene just to let the cops know what jerks they were. You can't believe how smooth it worked. Sharkey and me." His eyes were closed.

"Was this Halloween?"

"Listen, this was the payroll heist at the Unirubber Footwear, the biggest robbery ever happened in Mid-Hudson. Over two hundred thousand dollars. They looked for us in five different states. They sent the serial numbers all over the world. So we knew we had to wait to use that money."

"I want to know about Shirley Pendergast. Why, Anderson?"

Len opened his eyes but didn't seem to be seeing anything. His head was rolling away from his bleeding shoulder. "It's all in the footlocker, right where we put it. Up by Uncle Howard's shack, sixty-five feet from the big boulder by the creek. We did that. We were right here. All the time. We were right here." He focused his eyes and sat up a little: "I'm so tired. You shouldn't of taken my gun away."

"Anderson!" Max snapped. Len's head stopped lolling and his features gathered themselves into an expression of mild belligerence.

"Well, they canned him. Canned Ray. Sweetest man on earth. Pink slip, just like that. He was supposed to get married end of the month. I told him don't get mad, get even. All it takes is brains. See people get caught because they run. But we were right here. We were just like the Purloined Letter story we read in English class. A couple a hundred state police running all over and know where we were all day Saturday? Right there in the second basement. They never looked down there. Sitting in the dark, eating sandwiches and sleeping. Didn't leave till three next morning. Ray carried the money in a wastepaper sack. Sack's in the footlocker too. The cops had a dozen different people swearing they saw this, they saw that. They never even came close. Right, Ray?" He shook the lifeless leg. "We really did it, we really pulled it off."

"You're not making very much sense, Anderson. When was this?"

"Where you been? It was in the papers everywhere. It was on TV. They even called us The Untouchables 'cause of our masks and there was a huge stink about TV teaching people how to commit crimes. *Time* magazine wrote it up."

"You're saying you hid money that you stole on your uncle's land? So why did you murder Shirley Pendergast?"

The wound on Len Anderson's shoulder was congealing. He stared down at his spattered shirt and bloody hands with a look of innocent puzzlement. Then he screwed his face up craftily. "I was the one who figured it out. You get caught running or you get caught spending. You gotta be very careful not to screw things up after. How you gonna cover coming into all that bread in a little burg like Hargate? Suppose you wait all those years and then get nailed for income tax evasion? Not me, buddy. You gotta be careful, gotta look for the weak link in the chain; then you split up the money and pull up stakes, everybody split at the same time. Go some place where a man can have a private life. That's the whole point." He shivvered convulsively. "So the breeze can't ever touch you. So the thing's complete. Perfect all the way round. God, it's cold here. Go California. Someplace warm. Something's always tying me down. Spoils everything…. Ja' have a cigarette or something?"

Max took off his jacket and draped it loosely across Len's shaking shoulders. He took one of his cigars out, inserted it in the man's slack mouth and lit it.

"Shirley Pendergast?" Max asked again, wondering if the boy upstairs had called his aunt and who would get to them first: the family, the cops, or the doctor who was needed to stop this man's descent into ice-grey shock. Len's breathing was fast and shallow; he clutched at the cigar as if it held the magic that would save him.

"I know what to do." he whispered smokily. "But a guy like Sharkey—he was gonna brag. He'd spill the whole damn thing, soon as he had his hands on even a piece of it. All Ray did was drive, that's the thing of it. Dropped us off for the bust, picked us up next night exactly where I told him. While me and Sharkey sweat it out in the cellar, he was fishing in the Catskills, he was making good our alibi. Plan was so damn good, we never had to use it. Can you believe it? They questioned Ray about five minutes, tops. There were thirty others they'd laid off same time."

"Last week, Anderson. What happened last week?"

"I couldn't hold him. I swear to god, I couldn't keep

him cool. So finally he said we'll burn the place. At least that way she won't go have a swimming pool dug up. She'd never have been there at all but the old bastard had to go an' sell it. It was supposed to be mine. Everything spoils. But not this. This was perfect. There in the ground, in that footlocker. You know what I mean? We could get it anytime we was ready to split. Ray knows. Ray understands."

He had leaned back against Ray's legs. Tears slid out of the sides of his eyes. "Sweet Jesus I never thought she'd be in there. Screaming at us. With her arms hanging out that broken glass. She knew who we were. She was in there. Sharkey, Sharkey went in after her. Sweet *Jesus*, I'm still hearing it."

He moved his good hand softly against Ray's legs. "Got to hang on, Ray. So we don't screw it up. . . You know how smooth it worked."

Cars had come. Cars with flashing lights. Max walked down the aisle to let them in.

Coda

It was way past three when Max got back to Robby's place. There was a note for him on the floor which had been shoved under the door.

"Please telephone first thing in the morning. Mr. Rosen says absolutely no one is authorized to examine any of his files. He has no knowledge of anyone named Lee Sam.—Kent Brinkman."

Max went into Robby's bedroom and packed up his things. At this time of night he might get to Broome Street by 5:30. If he broke the speeding laws a time or two.

Betsy's face on the pillow was smooth, content, deep asleep. Pale whisps of hair at the top of her forehead curled sweetly. Max touched a strand with the barest tip of a finger; he didn't want to rouse her, he wanted to look at her face a moment and think of how it had looked earlier, mottled with ecstasy. He rolled over cautiously, putting his back against her body. She snuggled softly against it before relaxing back into total oblivion.

It was almost noon on a dark gray spring day. It must be chilly down here too. The radiator at the back of his painting studio which had needed adjusting all winter hissed sharply. Street noises from below did sound like a river going over rapids—Betsy was always saying the noise made her nostalgic for Wisconsin but he'd never heard it quite that way before. He studied the painting on the opposite wall—a grid in which colored rectangles hung in perfect balance, each movement checked by another. His body tightened and then twitched with his annoyance at it.

"I," Betsy muttered.

"Shhh, go back to sleep."

But he could tell from her body she did not. They both lay without moving for a number of minutes. "You know what's wrong with us, Max?" she said.

"You sound wide awake," he said.

"I'm thinking."

"You seem to be angry all the time." They'd done it again, speaking over each other at the same time.

Max rolled over and faced her. "I don't like my work," he said slowly.

Betsy looked frightened. He put his hand on her neck and stroked the skin.

"I'm so good at what I do I don't notice that it bores me. Don Juan is right. It's been boring me for quite a while."

"What do you want to do?"

"I dunno. Think a lot for starters. I don't know. You don't deal with a random world by taking an art vacation."

"I don't have a clue what you mean," she said, putting her arms around him. Her eyes clouded with worry. Her face drew up. It was fear, Max knew. And someone was knocking on their front door.

"Shhh," Betsy said, "they'll never know we're here."

"Birwhizzle, Birwhizzle!" The knocker was now shouting.

"Shit," said Max as the warmth left him.

"Iz very important! Mr. Birwhizzle. Open up there? Please!" The knocking continued.

Max sat up: "Come back *later*!"

"Mr. Birwhizzle, I must speak to you."

"*Later*!" Max yelled louder.

"Concerns your friend Rosen," the man insisted. He gave the door another urgent series of raps.

"Crap," Betsey said. "Tell him to wait 'til I'm decent at least." She scrambled down the ladder for her jeans and a shirt.

Max put on her bathrobe.

"Yeah," he said opening the door. "This is a hell of a..."

"Yes. I apologize very much for this intrusion. I'm Mr. Sam." He was a compact stocky man in a smartly tailored three-piece suit. His curly grey hair was clipped precisely around his oval skull. His grey-blue eyes were piercing and intense. There was a small grey moustache under his nose. He held a black briefcase in one hand and held the other out, formally, to be shaken. He radiated something wary and coiled and Max felt the energy of it in the tight, crisp handshake he accepted.

"You know I've been trying to reach you," Mr. Sam said.

"Look, you woke us up. I'm not in a state to talk reasonably, why don't you. . ."

"It is not always pozzible for me to observe all amenities. As I said, I apologize. It concerns some research undertaken by Mr. Rosen, research that has, how can I say, certain implications. I believe you are familiar wiz the nature of Rosen's inquiries?"

Betsy looked a little white. "You'd better come in, sit down and explain," she told him.

"Yesss thank you. You are familiar wiz them," he said

over his shoulder to Max as he followed Betsy to their kitchen table. It was a statement, not a question.

"Robby and I talk over lots of things. You'll have to tell me what you mean." Max let his testiness show. He gave Betsy the eye signals that meant don't offer this guy coffee.

"Heppmeyer." The man announced.

"No," Max lied.

"Yes," Mr. Sam said. He sat on one of the stools. "Helmut Ernst Heppmeyer." He gave a street address in Peekskill. "Fine bread. You visited the store and had an argument, Rosen waited in the car. Please. I have no time for games."

"Neither do I. Robby has no further interest in that man. But I can say he thinks Heppmeyer is an assumed name."

Mr. Sam nodded. "He has collected a dossier."

"He told me he's turned all his information over to the Israeli Mission to the U.N."

"He did not turn over papers."

"I don't know. Whatever, he told me they weren't particularly interested, so maybe they didn't accept them. The point is Rosen isn't interested any more. It was a mistake. His idea dead-ended. He writes fiction you know. He's always looking into possible stories."

"Nevertheless, a dossier was collected."

"What's your interest in this, Mr. Sam?"

"This is a sensitive business."

"I'm not particularly interested. And by the way, Robby doesn't know you. You told Marcia Jennings he does."

"You know as well as I do, Rosen is unavailable at the prezent. It is extremely important that I locate the dossier and correct information that was, was given to him in error."

"Look, you still haven't told me who you are. So all I know about you is you lied to a friend of mine. I think you've taken enough of my time."

"Mr. Birwhizzle, I think you're sophisticated enough to understand that allegations such as those made by your friend Rosen arouse interest in quarters that must operate with great discretion. Obviously, the government of the United States is not enthusiastic about operatives from other nations undertaking investigations of its residents yet it is often necessary to accomplish preliminaries independently, before cooperation is sought from proper authorities."

"Sounds terrific," Max growled. "Answer the question straight: Who the hell are you?"

"Lee Sam," he said. Mr. Sam unbuttoned the cuff of his tailored blue shirt pushing the sleeve up. He offered a white forearm with a vertical line of tattooed numbers extending in an uneven line up the inside of it. "I was born 7, November, 1921, Lodz, Poland. Name Leopold Saminski. In 1936 I was a rabbinical student. I have been many things since."

Max was ice: "Anyone can get a tattoo."

"Oh Max," Betsy interjected.

The man buttoned the cuff and readjusted his shirt and jacket sleeve without expression. "Dedicated amateurs provide us with invaluable assistance" he said. "But decisions about disposition of cases must be handled by those who understand the situation in its widest interpretation."

"There you go again," Max cut him off. "Who do you work for and what do you want?"

"I want to correct the documents and insure that they will be used wiz wisdom and discretion. I work for those who believe, as I do, that crimes against humanity muz be called to account, that they be made to further survival of intended victims, which is the highest justice. Do you have access to Rosen's dossier?"

"No, I don't. Your visit's over," Max stood up. "For all I know you're one of this Heppmeyer's creepy friends. They also look for the widest interpretation, I hear. Either way, I just don't give a damn. I'll tell you another thing— Rosen feels the exact same way and if you try harassing him, we'll go to the F.B.I. together and report all of this."

"With your background, you might be tempted to do so. Rosen, however, would never agree wiz you."

"What the hell kind of racial slur are you making?" Max could feel the red anger rising up his neck and flooding his face.

Lee Sam picked up his briefcase.

"Goddamn it!" Max roared. "Get out of my house!"

Betsy shut the door behind him.

"What?" she began when the locks were fastened.

"Robby's going to burn it," he said. "Betsy, I'm sorry," he choked, "leave me alone a minute."

She wants a baby. She wants me to want a baby. That's worse. What I want is to change my work. Maybe my whole life. It's not a puzzle with a beautifully balanced ending. It's not going to be as simple as helping Robbie make up his mind. He can either burn that notebook or give it to weird Mr. Sam. So what anyway? Shirley will still be dead, dead for nothing. Sharkey and Ray Walker are still dead too. I shouldn't have stopped Len Anderson from making a clean sweep of it, because what's ahead for him? Should I say so what to that too? I'll never play detective again, that I know. I'm seeing nothing but red.

MARTHA KING has never lived in the Hudson Valley or in SoHo where this story takes place. By the late 1970s, the time of this story, she was a matron in Brooklyn and with her mate, the artist Basil King, a parent of two half-grown daughters. She has written poetry, memoir, and short stories as well as writing for her former employers, Poets & Writers, Memorial Sloan-Kettering Cancer Center, and the National Multiple Sclerosis Society. This is her first novel.

For more see www.basilking.net

www.ingramcontent.com/pod-product-compliance
Lightning Source LLC
Chambersburg PA
CBHW050508190726
48284CB00003B/724